WHERE THE BODIES ARE BURIED

[signature]

KIM NEWMAN

[signature]

PETER ATKINS

[signature]

SYLVIA STARSHINE

[signature]

RANDY BROECKER

LIMITED EDITION

NUMBER *138* **OF** *500*

WHERE THE BODIES ARE BURIED

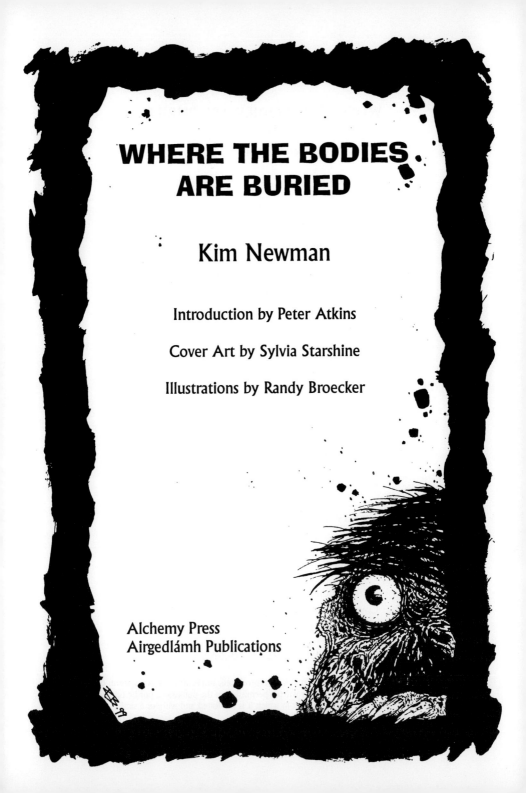

WHERE THE BODIES ARE BURIED

Kim Newman

Introduction by Peter Atkins

Cover Art by Sylvia Starshine

Illustrations by Randy Broecker

Alchemy Press
Airgedlámh Publications

WHERE THE BODIES ARE BURIED

Published in Great Britain by

THE ALCHEMY PRESS
46 Oxford Road, Acocks Green
Birmingham, B27 6DT, England

AIRGEDLÁMH PUBLICATIONS
130 Park View, Wembley
Middlesex, HA9 6JU, England

'Where the Bodies Are Buried'
First appeared in *Dark Voices 5* (Pan Books, 1993)
Edited by Stephen Jones and David Sutton

'Where the Bodies Are Buried II: Sequel Hook'
First appeared in *Dark Voices 6* (Pan Books, 1994)
Edited by Stephen Jones and David Sutton

'Where the Bodies Are Buried 3:
Black and White and Red All Over'
First appeared in *Dark Terrors* (Gollancz, 1995)
Edited by Stephen Jones and David Sutton

'Where the Bodies Are Buried 2020'
First appeared in *Dark Terrors 2* (Gollancz, 1996)
Edited by Stephen Jones and David Sutton

First edition

Introduction copyright © 2000 by Peter Atkins
Cover Art copyright © 2000 by Sylvia Starshine
Illustrations copyright © 2000 by Randy Broecker

ISBN 0-9532260-2-6

WHERE THE BODIES
ARE BURIED

CONTENTS

For Anne

INTRODUCTION

Peter Atkins

England, 1869. The poet and painter Dante Gabriel Rossetti knew where the body was buried. After all, he'd buried it. It was (or used to be) his wife, the former Elizabeth Siddall. Rossetti, as a final act of husbandly devotion upon her untimely passing seven years earlier, had folded into her dead hand the manuscripts – the only manuscripts – of many of his unpublished poems and buried them with her. Now, several texts short of a volume and with a publisher breathing down his neck, Rossetti had a tough decision to make. He made it. In one of the most famous acts of literary (and literal) grave robbing in the history of English Letters, he had Lizzie exhumed and the manuscripts retrieved. They were published the following year to great, albeit transitory, acclaim.

Kim Newman is a grave robber, too. And we should all be very grateful. Because Kim isn't digging up former spouses and stealing parting gifts to make himself a few bob: he's finding buried treasure. Or, in many cases, finding buried dross and, via the alchemy of his synthesising imagination, transforming it into gold.

Kim is one of our most skilled raiders of the collective unconscious, particularly those areas of it marked by the iconography of popular culture. His *Anno Dracula* books (three so far and more to come, I hope) are richly-detailed tapestries woven from a thousand histories, both real and fictional. *The Night Mayor,* his first novel, explores – with tremendous panache and finely-tuned narrative skills – a world populated by cyber-ghosts from the world of Film Noir. In his collaborations with Eugene Byrne (collected as *Back In The USSA),* characters we all know – and as disparate as Buddy Holly and The Likely Lads – appear in alternate incarnations, simultaneously charming us with the warmth of the familiar and thrilling us with the shock of the new.

One of the many pleasures of reading this strand of Kim's fiction is matching your own storehouse of memories against his – playing a kind of catch-the-reference-before he-explains-it game with the author. The good news is the game is open to anyone. The bad news is you'll nearly always lose. Kim will kick your ass. He just knows more about that shit than practically anyone else. If you're lucky enough to know Kim personally and have the balls for it, you can even play the game (or variants thereof) in the flesh. You should be warned, in fact, that Kim is *always* playing. No starting whistle. No half-time. If you're blathering on about some black-haired B-movie babe from fifties sci-fi then don't for Christ's sake confuse your Barbara Rushes with your Dana Wynters. Kim'll be all over you like Vinnie Jones in a Cup match. He shows no mercy and takes no prisoners. This stuff is important to him. Partly because, I suspect, it is so vitally important to his art. Indeed, on those extremely rare occasions when Kim does make a mistake, he is mortified beyond all reason. I remember him rushing up to me at a convention some years ago and referring to his recent in-print confusion of two Kurosawa movies in the tone of horrified and apologetic guilt that one traditionally reserves for telling your mate you got his sister pregnant and that you hope it won't affect her chances of promotion at the nunnery. I bought him a pint and did my best to help calm him down but I think the wound stayed open for days.

Kim is also, as many of you may know, a respected film critic and scholar. As well as his vituperatively entertaining reviews in various magazines, he is the author of *Nightmare Movies* and *Wild West Movies* and a contributor to and/or editor of several other reference books. The body of his critical work reveals that Kim is not only extremely knowledgeable about the films themselves but also of the muddied and confused circumstances in which the vast majority of films get made. He might, in the abstract, be as much of a sucker for the auteur theory as the rest of us but on a case-by-case basis he certainly seems refreshingly familiar with the chaos and compromise that are actually the parents of most celluloid babies. This knowledge is based, in part at least, on his own little adventures in the screen trade. Several of Kim's fictions have been optioned for movie adaptation and he's certainly suffered through his own share of pointless meetings, pinhead producers, and squandered opportunities, both in London and out here in Hollywood. Living and working here as I do, I've enjoyed considerably more day-to-day confrontations with the absurdities of The Development Process than Kim has but quantity isn't really the issue. The faces behind the desks may change but the platitudes, hidden agendas, and smiling lies (which, trust me, eventually flow freely from *both* sides of the desk) remain the same. And Kim's a smart guy. It doesn't take him long to learn.

Fortunately, it also doesn't take him long to recognise fertile ground for fiction. After all, we all know what the best fertiliser is, don't we? The stories you're about to read and enjoy – flowers of the imagination blossomed improbably from the dung of B-movie reality – first appeared episodically in anthologies edited by those worthy gentlemen Stephen Jones and David Sutton. Collected together here and illustrated by the remarkable Randy Broecker and Sylvia Starshine, they now form a long, albeit fractured, narrative. The book isn't exactly a novel but it's not exactly a collection either. In fact, what it reminds me of (and I hasten to add I'm not in any way referring to the book's quality) is the literary equivalent of one of those peculiarities of the 1960's – a theatrical movie cobbled together from various episodes of a TV series. The thought of form imitating content in that way brings a smile to my lips and I hope it will do the same for Kim because he's exactly the kind of bastard that could tell you precisely which episodes of *The Man From Uncle* were stitched together to give us *The Karate Killers*.

Peter *Atkins*
Los Angeles, March 1999

WHERE THE BODIES
ARE BURIED

In High Street, Robert Hackwill caught sight of his own name. It tugged the corner of his eye, drawing his attention. The elections were months past but his posters were still up in some places.

He stood in front of Valerie's Video, which he remembered as a junk and curio emporium. Ten years ago it became a video rental shop, then spread to encompass premises on either side, becoming a video super-rental shop. The added-on shop-fronts were boarded up and Valerie's was selling off used cassettes from £1.99. Only half the shop was devoted to videos, the rest boasting odd items from dusty fresh fruit to Nintendo cartridges. Video had been an eighties boom business.

The window was covered with glossy, saggy posters for films Hackwill wouldn't want Colin and Sammy to see. *Babes Bust Out*, with a pouting silicone freak in a shrunken T-shirt with prison arrows, brandishing a machine gun half her size, an out-of-focus exploding helicopter in the background. *Steam Heat II*, an 'erotic thriller' advertised by a buxom silhouette in a darkened bedroom raising a bloody trowel, the frightened eyes of the man beneath staring out from between the censor certificate and the credits block.

His election poster had been a nice black and white photograph of him, taken a year or so ago, before he got the slight flabbiness about his chin Helen was on at him to do something about. And 'VOTE HACKWILL'. No clever slogan, no promises: he was well enough known in town to stand on his reputation. Besides the Party had held his ward since before World War Two. He couldn't find the poster in Valerie's window, so he looked at the boarded-up shop next door. It had been fly-posted for jumble sales and discotheques. He was sure one of his posters had been up here, but it was either buried under more recent layers or shredded to strips.

He must have been mistaken. He felt silly, as if he'd been caught out. Then he looked back at the video posters and saw it. Bigger than the others and mainly black shadows with dripping red and green letters, it advertised a horror movie. Probably one of the video nasties he'd campaigned against a few years ago when everybody was worried about kiddies renting out snuff films. A single red eye, stark mad, stared out of the shadowed ruin of a face, a double-row of shining teeth clenched and exposed in a lipless mouth. A withered hand, fingers tipped with steel claws, seemed to reach out of the poster, each shiny claw containing the screaming face of a teenage boy or girl. Underneath was an abandoned graveyard, tombstones leaning at bizarre angles, weeds growing up around forgotten monuments.

At the top of the poster were the words 'Rob Hackwill Knows...', and, in bigger letters like razor-slashes in velvet, the title of the film, *Where the Bodies Are Buried*. He looked again, assuming he'd mistaken something similar for his name. Rod Bicknell, Don Treadwell, Jack Robwill? No, it was definitely 'Rob Hackwill'. Most people called him Robert. Only Helen and a few of his oldest friends, and enemies, called him Bob, even. But Rob Hackwill was unmistakably a variation of his name.

He detected, for the first time, the possibility of a cruel joke. And if cruel jokes were involved, the obvious suspect was the Independent. Reg Jessup, a sitting councillor, had left the Party and stood again on his own ticket, besting the official candidate to be returned as more of a nuisance than the actual opposition. Elaborate and pointless jokes were a hobby of his. Reg's entire political career was an elaborate and pointless joke.

He stormed into Valerie's, sounding the bell, and cringed. By the counter was a cardboard cut-out of a small blonde woman in karate pyjamas, aiming a kick somewhere in the vicinity of Hackwill's head, mouth open in an intimidating silent yell.

'Don't mind her,' said another blonde, a girl whose hair was bleached almost white. She sat on a high stool behind the counter, dressed all in black and reading a film magazine. 'She's just an ad for *Foxy Kickboxer*.'

The girl thumbed over her shoulder, indicating a television high up on a shelf, sound turned low. The original of the cut-out, less imposing when shrunk into the tiny box, exploded out of a Jacuzzi, pyjamas plastered over prominent nipples, and launched punches into a half-dozen Asians. They had swords but she saw them off with just her hands and feet, and, in one case, her breasts.

'Not exactly Wim Wenders,' said the girl, 'but there's a market for it.'

He didn't know the girl. She wasn't Valerie, whose real name was Jeanie

Morris. Hackwill had met Jeanie when the council reprimanded her for renting 18 certificate films to sixteen-year-olds.

'I'm Robert Hackwill,' he announced.

The girl's dead-white brow wrinkled and she looked at him as if he had declared himself the Prime Minister or Ken Dodd.

'I want an explanation.'

'Rob Hackwill?'

'Robert. Mr Hackwill. Councillor Hackwill. And I want to know why you're defaming me in your window.'

The girl burst out laughing and covered her mouth with glossy black fingernails.

Dust from the building site drifted across Denbeigh Gardens along with the battering drone of pneumatic drills. When Hackwill found himself coughing, Reg gave him a matey back-thump, harder than necessary. He had to grip hard to keep hold of his briefcase.

'Get those lungs clear, Bob,' he said. 'I thought you'd kicked ciggies into touch, old thing.'

Hackwill coughed against his free fist, knowing his face was burning red. The man from the *Herald* was taking photographs. He was sure the paper would pick the worst-looking one of him, as usual, to go with the story.

Next to the grassy triangle of Denbeigh Gardens rose the skeleton of the Discount Development. It should've been finished six months ago, but there'd been cock-ups since Day One. Hackwill had worked closely with the McKinnell Brothers from the beginning. His firm was supplying many of the materials. It was a plank of his campaign that the Development would be an invigorating economic injection for the area. His family economy was certainly invigorated; the Brothers' generous 'consultation fees' were putting Sammy through junior school.

As Ben McKinnell, almost spherical in his shell-suit, explained to the reporter about the set-backs, Reg smirked at each lengthy anti-union aside. Reg said if you put a penny in the slot, any McKinnell Brother would give out a five-minute tirade about the tyranny of work-shy yobs.

Lucia Howell, the Opposition leader, tottered on high heels, peering at neglected flowerbeds as if she took this inspection lark seriously. One of her ever-present St Bernards rooted around somewhere, getting underfoot.

Denbeigh Gardens was council property but nothing much had ever been done with it. The playground consisted of two lethal swings and a concrete lump supposedly in the shape of a whale, its flapping tail broken off by vandals. There was a shed, reputedly locked since the turn of the century, marked with a 'Council Property: Keep Out' notice. Denbeigh Gardens would be no loss. Hackwill could force the sale through but it would be easier if the decision were unanimous.

Ben McKinnell, questioned, admitted the original plans had under-estimated the parking space necessary for the Development and that he was more than willing to pay a good price for the Gardens.

Hackwill looked across the area. Kids played tag around the mutilated whale. Their young mothers loitered by the shed, using it as a windbreak while they lit cigarettes. He wished he hadn't given up. Brickies on their tea break whistled and called at the smoking girls, receiving only snooty looks and rude gestures. McKinnell joked that he wanted to send his builders on an Anti-Sexism Awareness course, and Jilly Kenner, Hackwill's militant deputy, commented that being arse-raped a couple of times might improve their attitude.

'Right on, Jilly,' said Reg. He always backed anything that made the Party look like loons.

'Excuse me, Councillor Hackwill?'

He turned and saw a tweedy young woman in glasses.

'I'm Ginger Dillon, from the Denbeigh Residents' Committee.'

Hackwill remembered the name. She'd written many letters, complaining. Mrs Dillon was a NIMBY; in favour of the Discount Development, but Not In My Back Yard.

'We're petitioning against the loss of this park area.'

Mrs Dillon handed him a substantial folder of signatures. Hackwill heard the click of the *Herald* man's camera and saw Reg's grin widen. He had suspicions that this had been stage-managed.

'There has been consultation with the residents at every stage of the Development,' said Ben McKinnell, waving a fat cigar. 'Mrs Dillon represents a minority opinion.'

Hackwill found himself with the petition in one hand and his briefcase in the other. Another cloud of dust whisked past and he coughed again, this time racked with convulsions. He dropped case and folder, and bent double. Reg hit his back again. Lucia scrambled to pick up the petition and huddled with Mrs Dillon. The NIMBY had been an Opposition candidate at the last election. Unsuccessful, thank Christ. Reg, Jilly and Lucia were quite enough.

Hackwill cleared his lungs and straightened up. Reg brushed his shoulders like a valet, solicitous for his health. The Independent had been the same in school thirty years ago. He had a way of seeming to be a friend while actually making you look bad. Sometimes, Hackwill wished they were back in Ash Grove Primary, where direct methods could end a dispute. District Councillors weren't allowed to give Chinese Burns.

Reg had Hackwill's briefcase, upside-down. As he handed it over, the catch broke and things fell out. He made a grab for the plain brown folder with his consultancy invoices, certain the *Herald* reporter would make a sudden grab for the evidence and Hackwill would find himself indicted, shamed and forced to resign. There was nothing illegal in being paid for a job well done, but he knew how it would look if it came out.

'What's this, Bob?' Reg asked, holding up the cassette box, 'taking home a pervy video?'

He opened the black box and read the title.

'*Where the Bodies Are Buried*. Sounds gruesome. I had you down as more a *Chariots of Fire* sort of chap.'

Hackwill didn't want to explain why he'd rented the tape. It would make him look ridiculous.

'For the kids,' he said.

'But,' the grin infected Reg's entire face, 'this has an 18 certificate. I'm sure Colin isn't fourteen yet and Sammy is just a baby.'

Hackwill snatched the video and stuffed it into his case along with all the papers. The invoices were safely buried at the bottom.

'When can we expect the council's decision?' asked the reporter.

Hackwill had to concentrate.

'About the car park?' the man from the *Herald* prompted.

Mrs Dillon glared like a witch. Ben McKinnell exhaled smoke, which dissipated on the breeze.

'Next Tuesday,' Hackwill replied. 'We'll discuss it fully in council, and, if there's any disagreement, put it to a vote.'

'How did you like the film?' asked the neo-albino girl, whose name was Shelley.

Hackwill harrumphed about it being rubbish. Bloody rubbish, to be precise. Shelley had to bend down low to put the film back in the W section behind the counter and her short black skirt rode up.

'It's a popular rental,' she said.

When Colin had discovered his Dad had taken out *Where the Bodies Are Buried*, he wanted to be allowed to watch the video. All his friends had seen it and it was supposed to be wicked. Apparently, there was a scene where a boy's eyeballs crawled out of his head and strangled him with trails of optic nerve. Also, Colin helpfully informed his father, the baddie had their surname, Hackwill. He sent Colin and Sammy to bed and put the tape on. After the first five minutes, in which a girl was attacked in a graveyard by a monster with one red eye, Helen gave him a funny look and went upstairs too.

Shelley slipped the video in its place and stood up. She smoothed her skirt, giving him a shop assistant smile. She was the age of the girls in the film, the girls chased and killed by the monster, Rob Hackwill.

He'd watched most of *Where the Bodies Are Buried* on fast-forward, going to regular speed when anyone was murdered or, looking around to make sure Helen wasn't back, whenever a teenager took off her clothes. There was no story, just a series of freakish deaths. During one of the murders, the victim – a fat gangster with a cigar stub permanently in his mouth – shouted 'get back, Hackwill' as the monster advanced. Then his cigar turned into dynamite and exploded, making a fireball of his head. Hackwill played it over twice, to make sure. The fat man definitely said 'Hackwill'.

While on fast-forward, he'd come to a scene without a murder or sex, when the heroine visited a middle-aged man played by someone he remembered as a Sheriff in a seventies TV show. He decided to watch properly, hoping there'd be an explanation. The Sheriff was a Judge in *Where the Bodies Are Buried*, and the heroine, a disturbingly mature schoolgirl named Tina, was his granddaughter. Her parents and most of her friends had been killed, and the Judge knew something.

'Rob Hackwill,' the Judge sighed, voice heavy with dread. 'He's come back.'

Hackwill had shivered. He didn't understand why people paid good money to be frightened.

'Rob Hackwill?' pouted Tina, who was unlikely to give Meryl Streep nightmares at Oscar-time. 'I've heard that name somewhere before.'

The Judge nodded and shook his head. 'You must have been very little when it happened, the suicides, the scandal...'

The picture went wavy and the Judge's voice continued to explain while pictures showed a mob chasing a one-eyed man into the graveyard.

'He was a blackmailer,' the Judge said. 'A vicious, evil blackmailer. He had an uncanny knack for ferreting out secrets, for inflating innuendoes into slanders, for discovering where the bodies were buried. For years, he preyed on the town, turning people against one another, ruining lives, wrecking marriages. Everyone came to dread the anonymous poison letters. Everyone with a secret.'

The mob, led by the fat gangster and the Judge, cornered the cringing man. He was the actor who played the monster, without make-up. He fell exhausted against a gravestone and begged for his life.

'We found out it was Rob Hackwill. He'd been a councilman until we indicted him for taking graft from the Mob. The letters had been his revenge. He hadn't done it for the money. It had all been to ruin the city.'

The gangster had a blowtorch. He advanced on the blackmailer, belly looming over the camera.

'That night,' the Judge said, 'we tortured him, trying to find where he had stashed the evidence he used against us. He wouldn't talk but we kept on torturing him until there was no point torturing him any more. We left him with the other dead things, thinking we had heard the last of Rob Hackwill. But now...'

The film came back to the Judge, who held his head in his hands. Tina was looking at him, disgusted.

'But now he's come back.'

The lights went out and when they came back the Judge's tongue inflated to the size of a watermelon, bursting his head like a pimple. Tina screamed as the Judge's head stretched and split. The camera whirled around, and standing in front of the French windows was the monster.

Rob Hackwill.

Hackwill froze the frame and looked at his namesake. The poison penman had made a bargain with the Devil, a dark woman in a black leather body-stocking. He could come back to life, providing he regularly delivered souls to his mistress in Hell. He lived in a cavern under the graveyard and had one red eye, shining bare teeth and steel claws. When he killed someone, he said something funny. Hackwill unfroze the frame. 'That was the trouble with the Judge,' the monster said, 'his tongue always wrote cheques his ass couldn't cash.'

He'd fast-forwarded through the rest of the film: Tina summoned up the Devil who, changing her mind, dragged the monster back to Hell, where he was torn apart by the ghosts of his victims. In the last scene, Tina was back in a depopulated school, shaken but a survivor. She went to the ladies for a smoke and a black shape with a glowing red eye burst out of a toilet bowl, filling the screen. Heavy metal played over the rising end credits.

'The sequel is supposed to be worse,' Shelley said.

'There's a sequel?'

She shrugged. 'There's always a sequel.'

'You've got it?'

He didn't want to rent the film, just look at the box. All morning, he hadn't been able to get the bits of *Where the Bodies Are Buried* he had seen out of his head.

'It's not on video yet. It's not even been at the Palace.'

Shelley dug through a pile behind the counter and found a film magazine. She paged through it until she came to an advert.

'Here,' she said.

It was a scrambling of the video poster, the same elements in a different order. The red eye, the claws, the graveyard, the jagged teeth, the screaming teenagers.

Where the Bodies Are Buried, Part II: Hackwill's Back!

'I'll bet you can't wait,' Shelley said. 'It must be fun having everybody be afraid of you.'

Because Reg and Jilly abstained, the Denbeigh Gardens vote was deadlocked. It was not a Party issue. One of the Opposition, who owned a delivery firm connected with the McKinnell Brothers, voted for the sale. But, under the influence of Mrs Dillon, Lucia had taken against it, so no decision could be made. There was nothing more to be done in this meeting. As chairman, he sat facing everyone. At the other end of the table, the Reg Jessup grin shone. Hackwill thought he heard Reg's suppressed chortle.

'Does anyone wish to change their vote?'

Hackwill looked at Jilly, hoping she'd turn around and toe the Party Line for once. If Ben McKinnell hadn't made that joke about Anti-Sexism

Awareness, he might have a better chance of getting a proper car park.

Reg was abstaining just to stir things up. He had been the one who delivered the McKinnell Brothers' proposition to him in the first place. As usual, he had set everything in motion and backed off.

No one wanted to change.

'We have to make a decision.'

'If it's an even split,' a clerk said, 'surely, the motion falls...'

'Perhaps we stay here until someone cracks,' Reg suggested.

Hackwill drummed his fingers on the table. Looking down, he noticed he'd scratched the veneer. His nails were too long. He must cut them.

He'd hoped he could just go into the Palace, buy a ticket and hide in the auditorium, but for the first time in years there was a queue. Hackwill had told Helen he'd be home late because of another committee meeting. There was a cut-out in the foyer. Rob Hackwill, the monster. The cut-out was about his size and the red eye lit up electrically. Hackwill couldn't look at his namesake.

The queue was mainly excited young people. He was sure most weren't old enough to see the film. They were blithely unaware that they were breaking the law, but he, well above the legal age for an 18 film, was the one skulking guiltily, hoping no one would notice him.

'Come to see yourself?' someone asked.

Bewildered, he turned, heart thumping. It was Shelley, in a floor-length black dress slit up the thighs. She was with a boy who wore eye-shadow.

'Chris, this is the real Rob Hackwill,' she told her boyfriend. 'Remember, I told you about him.'

The boy smiled, showing sharp eye-teeth.

'Robert,' he insisted. 'Not Rob.'

'You must be becoming a horror expert,' Shelley said. 'You'll be subscribing to *Fangoria* next.'

'Pardon?'

'He didn't think much of *Where the Bodies Are Buried*,' Shelley told Chris.

The boy shrugged. 'I thought it was overrated too,' he said. He had an educated voice, a bit posey. 'Allan Keyes betrayed his own story. His vision is way too weird to be hammered into a commercial package...'

'Keyes?'

'Allan Keyes is the director,' Shelley explained. 'He's better known as a writer. You must have seen his books. *Strange Segments*, *Busting a Gut*, *Cornworld...*'

'Did he make this too?' Hackwill asked, nodding at the poster for *Hackwill's Back*.

'No,' Chris said, 'he got shafted by Hollywood. Sold away the rights for a mess of Beverly Hills pottage.'

'It must be like being locked out of your own house,' Shelley said, 'having your life's work taken away from you.'

'This is directed by the woman who made the Putrid promos.'

The queue started moving and Hackwill got a ticket. He had to exchange an embarrassed greeting with the cinema manager, who he knew from some committee or other, before he was allowed into the auditorium. The manager was surprised to see him, but he didn't bother to find an excuse.

'Rob Hackwill?' said the manager. 'Funny, I'd never thought of it before. Odd coincidence, eh?'

He finally escaped into the dark and sat near the back. Shelley and Chris were down in the front row. As the lights went down for the trailers, he saw them kissing and imagined their tongues entwining like slithering snakes, knotting their heads together.

The main character of *Where the Bodies Are Buried, Part II* was Frankie, a teenage boy whose penis was cursed by Rob Hackwill and turned from time to time into a toothy snake. In one scene, the condition came upon him while he was screwing the school slut. The snake ate its way out of the girl, splattering Frankie with her insides.

Days later, Hackwill remembered the scene with a chill. Knowing it was all special effects, rubber and ketchup and complicated electronic gadgets, did not help.

In the Town Hall Gents, he looked down at his own penis. He'd drunk several cups of tea and his bladder was uncomfortably full. He remembered Frankie's trouser snake and could not let his bladder go. It was agonising. Behind him, someone coughed. He turned, zipping up sharply, and smelled cigar smoke. Ben McKinnell stood by the hand-drier.

'Councillor Hackwill,' he said. 'About the vote...'

'No change, I'm afraid.'

The developer shrugged. 'We'll have to play a rougher game.'

Years ago, when the McKinnell Brothers were starting out, there were stories about a shop steward whose hands got broken.

Ben McKinnell gave him a large brown envelope. 'Councillor Howell might be persuaded to change her vote.'

'Lucia? Not likely.'

'Open the envelope.'

He did and slid out a sheaf of black and white photographs, eight by ten like film stills.

'Taken with a telephoto lens,' Ben McKinnell explained. 'That's why they're a bit grainy.'

Lucia Howell was an animal-lover. With her husband Quentin, she was known for breeding show-dogs. Her mantel-piece was crowded with trophies and ribboned medals. They could be seen in the background of the photographs. Lucia and Quentin were recognisable, as were their prize-winning St Bernards: Courage, Missy and Big Brute. Hackwill had not realised how much of an animal-lover the Opposition leader was, or how enthusiastically her husband, a gentleman farmer, joined her in her hobby.

Tea still sloshing inside him, Hackwill left the Gents. Ben McKinnell ducked out and left the Town Hall.

Lucia was in the corridor outside the committee room. She had Big Brute with her. His tongue flopped to the floor as she scratched his abundant neck-fur, cooing in his large ear.

'Lucia,' he began, 'could I have a word before the meeting. Something has come up.'

Mrs Dillon had found his home number and called dozens of times, leaving stinging messages with Helen and, in one case, Sammy. When he got in, he had to take one of her calls. It was surprisingly painless, since he was able to divert the NIMBY bile towards Lucia.

After the vote, he'd felt an enormous sense of release. For one thing, his bladder let go. For another, Lucia's change of vote encouraged several Opposition councillors to follow suit. The sale of Denbeigh Gardens went through. Then Reg lowered his voice to sound like the gravelly American who narrated horror film trailers and comically snarled 'Hackwill's Back!'

The Independent couldn't know exactly how he'd influenced Lucia but Hackwill realised Reg did understand. They had known each other too long and could keep nothing hidden. At school Reg had been the look-out, watching for teachers while Hackwill snatched some snotnose's dinner money. He had got his jollies being part of it without getting his hands dirty.

Hackwill tucked into his bacon and beans with relish. Since the meeting, he'd not thought of *Where the Bodies Are Buried*, parts I or II. The monster had brushed his life and was now speeding back to Hell, never to be heard from again.

'Turn the telly off,' Helen told Colin, 'and come have your tea.'

Hackwill looked across the kitchen into the front room. Colin was squatting by the television set.

'After the bweak,' Jonathan Ross said, 'we'll be talking to the most fwightening man in the world...'

He knew what the chat-show host would say.

'Wob Hackwill.'

Mal Gariazzo, the actor under the Rob Hackwill rubberface, was a volatile little American who barely let Ross get out a question before getting into his flow. He talked about Rob Hackwill as a mythic archetype, as an aspect of the Jungian Unconscious, and movie monsters as the demons of the modern pantheon.

'In a very real sense, Jonathan,' Gariazzo concluded, 'our society *needs* Rob Hackwill.'

Helen clapped ironically. She'd heard about Rob Hackwill the movie monster somewhere but not thought it interesting enough to discuss with her husband. Now her only comment was that she realised why he'd brought home that horrid video a few weeks ago.

It wasn't as if Robert Hackwill were a common name. He'd never come across another Hackwill to whom he was not related, let alone another *Robert* Hackwill.

Fascinated, he watched Gariazzo rattle on. In an open-necked striped shirt and leather trousers, the actor was very unlike the dead-faced monster, but he did the deep and scary Rob Hackwill voice when prompted.

The television showed a clip from *Part II*. Rob Hackwill spoke to Frankie from the cover of the Satanic Heavy Metal LP the teenager played backwards to bring the monster back from Hell. 'You and me, bro,' the monster said, 'we're gonna tear down this graveyard town and cover it with asphalt. Their lives will be our parking lot.'

Ross asked Gariazzo whether Allan Keyes, the creator of Rob Hackwill, would be participating in further sequels. The actor deftly skipped the question. Hackwill recognised the trick from meetings: it always came when someone didn't want to deal with a point raised by a report.

'We've already done *Where the Bodies Are Buried, Part III in 3-D*,' Gariazzo said. 'Rob Hackwill will be badder than ever. Straight from Hell to a Theatre Near You, he'll be slashing and snipping, getting close to your heart and deep into your pulsating brain.'

Ross shut the actor up and introduced a pop group. Five poofs with squeaky voices who Sammy thought were outstanding.

'Excellent,' said Colin, 'My Dad From Hell.'

Without thinking, Hackwill cuffed his son. The blow landed harder than intended and Colin was knocked over. Helen drew in a sharp breath.

'Bob,' she said, 'he's bleeding.'

He looked at his fingers and saw drops of red at the points of his nails. Colin, frightened, scrambled away. Helen, shocked, extended her hands as if to protect herself. Hackwill hissed through bared teeth.

Hackwill dreamed he was in Hell, his face being stripped of skin and flesh by a white-haired girl demon.

When he woke up, his left eye wouldn't open. It was sleep-gummed and no amount of warm water would do anything for it. In the end, Helen shrugged and said it was bound to come unstuck eventually and that he shouldn't worry about it too much.

Looking at himself with one eye in the mirror, he thought his face was tighter, more shrunken. And his right eye was rimmed with red as if he were a heavy drinker.

'Since you stopped smoking, you've become a wreck, Rob,' Helen said.

'Bob,' he corrected.

'Pardon?'

'My name is Bob.'

'That's what I said, Bob.'

'No, you said Rob. Like the monster, Rob. Not Bob, like the husband.'

She left him in the bathroom, examining his face. His eye still wouldn't open.

'Get used to it, Rob,' he told himself.

Reg was in his office to give him the news about the Howells. Their Land Rover had gone off a bridge. They were both dead.

'Looks like they lost control,' Reg said, keeping the gloating to a minimum. 'But the police are puzzled by one detail.'

Reg let it dangle, until Hackwill snapped a question. 'What?'

'The dogs. There's no evidence of a break-in, so it looks like Lucia and Quentin did it themselves.'

'Did what?'

'Killed their dogs. With a carving knife. Those St Bernards were like their children, but...'

Hackwill was uncomfortable. The photographs Ben McKinnell had given him were locked in the filing cabinet. He'd have to destroy them.

'Bob, is there something wrong with your eye?'

He thought he should be there to see the ground broken. It was the first really hot day of the summer and the bulldozer driver's bare belly flopped over his jeans belt as he sat at the wheel, starting up his machine. A few stood at the perimeter of Denbeigh Gardens, watching. At least the NIMBYs weren't staging a human chain.

Hackwill could imagine Mrs Dillon going down under the blades, sliced up and redistributed like the dummies of the *Where the Bodies Are Buried* films, entrails spread like bright streamers in the marks of caterpillar tracks.

The bulldozer growled across the park, scraping away grass. The wedge-shovel ploughed against the concrete whale and broke it up, sweeping the chunks aside. The swings crumpled as if they were made from paper straws. On the return pass, the machine smashed down the ancient hut. It proved completely empty.

There was a brief pause when the driver saw something white in the earth and thought it might be a human thigh-bone. Ben McKinnell pronounced it a piece of a cow and tossed it away. The levelling of Denbeigh Gardens continued.

Underneath the grass, there was only soft earth.

He was late for the meeting. As he entered the room, someone growled 'Hackwill's Back' in a horror film accent. Reg didn't even have to do it himself now. It was a standing joke.

There had been a snap election to fill the empty place on the council and somehow Ginger Dillon had been selected by the Opposition. She was a one-issue councillor and her pet peeve was the Discount Development. Every time Hackwill sat in his chair at the head of the table, Mrs Dillon pulled out more press cuttings and statistics, coming perilously close to libelling everyone concerned with the Development from the McKinnell Brothers down to the site tea-boy.

Even before the minutes of the last meeting could be read, Mrs Dillon was waving documents that proved Douggie McKinnell had been fined for bribing a borough surveyor in the next county.

'These people are no better than gangsters, Mr Chairman, and we've let them have the run of town.'

Hackwill was tired. His sleep had been troubled recently. Helen and the kids were treating him strangely. Also, he knew that sooner or later he would sit down in council and Mrs Dillon would raise the matter of consultancy fees.

'The Development is nearly a year overdue, with no end in sight. I propose we suspend our relationship with the McKinnells and reassess our whole position.'

Hackwill looked at Mrs Dillon with his one red eye and tried by sheer force of will to shut her up. A sound started in his stomach and vibrated up through his teeth.

Somewhat alarmed, the woman paused in mid-rant and cringed back into her seat. Everyone else was similarly stunned. Good. It was time he reaffirmed his control over the situation.

'That's better,' Hackwill hissed. 'Any other business?'

The publicity for *Where the Bodies Are Buried, Part III in 3-D* began months before the film came to the cinemas. Little boxes in every newspaper and magazine Hackwill picked up bore messages: 'He Knows, Be Scared', 'In Your Face, Rob Hackwill' and 'The Hack is Comin' Back!' Rob Hackwill was everywhere: posters, pop records, T-shirts, comics, paperback books, Halloween masks, Christmas Tree ornaments. The monster was impossible to escape. Hackwill understood from Shelley that each film made more money than the last and that each new sequel boosted video rental of earlier titles.

Every once in a while, he would drop in to Valerie's Video to check up on the snowballing Rob Hackwill craze. Shelley, the only person in town who didn't show either fear or contempt in his presence, was helpful, and collected articles from horror film magazines for him. She'd had a row with Chris, and the project filled her suddenly-available free time.

When Jeanie Morris judged one of the rental cassettes of the original *Where the Bodies Are Buried* battered enough to be sold off to make room for new stock, Shelley kept it back for Hackwill. He felt obliged to cough up the £1.99 for the film that had somehow become a piece of his life. The only other videos he owned were a collection of his own appearances on the local news, taped off the television, and Elvis and Ann-Margaret in *Viva Las Vegas*, which Colin had given him for his birthday last year.

Shelley sorted through her stack of papers and cuttings, searching out something for him. She was taking time off between college and university, and hoped to study film at East Anglia. She subscribed to a raft of film magazines, as interested in the ones with pictures of a grinning Rob Hackwill on the cover and disgusting colour stills of mutilated bodies inside as she was in the ones with no illustrations and huge wedges of incomprehensible text littered with footnotes and references. Personally, she preferred black and white films, which Hackwill thought might be why she dressed only in black – down to her lipstick – and had such white skin and hair. He could not imagine Shelley with a suntan.

There were Rob Hackwill cut-outs all over Valerie's Video. He caught sight of his reflection in the glass of the window. Among the Rob Hackwill shapes, he lurked, his red eye and bared teeth matching their rictus expressions. He had developed the habit of drawing his lips away from his teeth and hissing. His hand was given to locking into a clenched claw too. He supposed it must be psychosomatic.

All over town, his old election posters were reappearing, surgically altered to overlay the characteristics of the monster on his face. Usually, one eye was obscured and the other coloured red, and a gash of teeth were drawn over his smile. Written across 'VOTE HACKWILL' was the scrawl 'or he'll kill you!'

'Here's the piece I was telling you about,' Shelley said, handing over several photocopied sheets clipped together. 'It's by that bloke who used to be on Channel 4. An analysis of the whole Rob Hackwill phenomenon. It gets woolly towards the conclusion, but there's meat in the text.'

The Channel 4 fellow began by dissecting the name 'Rob Hackwill' –

'"Rob": to steal, a crime; "Hack": to maim, a lowlife; "Will": the force of determination, a power of the mind' – then followed the changes Keyes had made between 'A Trickle of Shame', his original short story, and *Where the Bodies Are Buried*, the first film. The author suggested Rob Hackwill had escaped from Allan Keyes, growing into a different kind of character. In the story, the monster, who didn't even have a name, was simply an incarnation of the guilts that prey on the characters. In *Where the Bodies Are Buried*, Rob Hackwill, thanks to Mal Gariazzo and some touches of black humour, had somehow become an engaging personality for the film's predominantly teenage audience. Rob Hackwill was 'at once the true face of evil behind the hypocrisy of his older generation and the anarchic trouble-maker who brings down the corrupt figures – fathers, judges, policemen, mob bosses – who represent the small-town setting.'

Hackwill had to struggle to weed out the meaning of the article, and felt he knew no more at the end than at the start. The point seemed to be that there were many Rob Hackwills. He supposed he was one of them.

'Rob,' Reg said – everyone called him Rob now – hovering over his desk, 'have you noticed that no matter how hot it gets, Mrs Dillon doesn't wear short-sleeved blouses. But you can see blue marks through her sleeves. What do you make of them? D'you reckon hubby gives her a bit of a belt?'

He shook his head. No, Mr Dillon didn't hit his wife. There was no Mr Dillon any more. He had left the bitch last year, and Hackwill knew why. He couldn't take her Problem any longer.

Her Surprising Problem.

He hadn't needed a McKinnell to find out. He'd managed on his own. He'd discovered he was good at finding things out. Sometimes, Reg hinted at things to help him, but mainly he did things on his own.

'One thing about Ginger,' Hackwill said, 'she's certainly been a shot in the arm.'

Reg laughed out loud but Hackwill could tell he was scared as well as pleased. He must have a Secret too. Everybody did.

Allan Keyes didn't give many interviews, but he had made an exception for the leading American horror film magazine. Shelley left Hackwill a message on his ansaphone telling him she was photo-copying the piece for him.

When he played the message back, Reg was still hanging around his office.

'Allan Keyes, eh?' he said. 'Who'd have thought it?'

'What?'

'I suppose it must be the same Allan Keyes.'

Hackwill looked at Reg, and felt his eye burning under the patch. Reg was being especially infuriating.

'We were all kids together. Now he's in Hollywood and we're still stuck here in the old town.'

'Do you mean to say we knew this Keyes?'

Reg laughed.

'More you than me, Robbo.'

Most of the interview was about Allan Keyes's reconciliation with New Frontier, the company that made the *Where the Bodies Are Buried* films. He had signed away all rights to the story and characters in exchange for the chance to direct and rumours had been circulating that he was unhappy with the way the sequels had been handled. He said Rob Hackwill had become too clownish, too obvious. He wasn't scary any more, and there was too much Heavy Metal in the films. Now, after the stalling of a big studio project, Keyes was returning to the series, providing an original storyline for *The Redevelopment: Where the Bodies Are Buried IV*.

Hackwill looked at the photocopied photograph of Keyes inset into the text. The face was bleached to white, the eyes holes in the picture, a razor-cut fringe of black hair indistinguishable from the background. Nothing in the reproduced and degraded image reminded him of anyone he could consciously remember. The article was entitled 'The Man Who Created Rob Hackwill', and illustrated with scratchy sketches, by Keyes himself, of his early ideas of the character.

Mal Gariazzo, whose death-by-hanging had been ruled 'due to sexual adventure' by the Hollywood coroner, would obviously have to be replaced. Keyes, who was fulsome in his praise for the late actor, promised that a new face would mean a new Rob Hackwill, a more serious monster for the nineties. 'No crappy jokes,' he promised, 'just no-frills scares.' The new film would 'explore the Rob Hackwill mythos', and finally explain that the whole curse was due to the fact that the town's founders had built on an

Indian burial ground. 'Rob Hackwill is white America, the parasite,' Keyes explained, 'the cancer on the virgin land, the epitome of the 20th Century nightmare.'

At the end, the interviewer asked the question Hackwill had been waiting for. 'Where did the name come from?'

'It's kind of silly,' Keyes said. 'When I was a kid in England, there was a bully in my playground...'

'Remember when you made him drink water from the toilet?' Reg said. 'And the time you hung his shorts from the climbing frame after PE? You were a right little monster, Robbo.'

Hackwill still could remember almost nothing.

Ben McKinnell told him there was another set-back, and no more capital was available for the Discount Development. Hackwill fixed the developer with his eye and made demands. McKinnell countered with threats. Certain deals could be made public. He chewed his cigar stub and Hackwill was reminded of the gangster in *Where the Bodies Are Buried*, the one whose head catches fire.

McKinnell inhaled and began to cough. Hackwill made no move to help him. The cigar fell, and smouldered on the carpet. McKinnell's face was red, and his hands were around his own throat. He looked as if he were throttling himself.

Hackwill hissed through his teeth.

The developer fell off his chair and crawled a few feet before turning on his back, eyes staring up. Ben McKinnell had swallowed his own tongue and choked on it.

Hackwill made and unmade a clawed fist.

Who'd have believed it? He chortled to himself, his nails rapping the table.

Ginger Dillon was a heroin addict, nearly bankrupt because of her habit. Jilly Kenner, the feminist, had paid for her university tuition as a nude model. The publisher of the *Herald* had a taste for underage girls and had stopped running editorials making 'Rob Hackwill' jokes. Jeanie Morris kept a selection of hard-core pornography under the counter for special customers and was willing to turn over her client list to keep the secret safe. His own secretary had two abortions before her sixteenth birthday and another one on the way. The chair of the housing committee had three bank accounts under assumed names. Douggie McKinnell had killed a business rival with a cricket bat. The manager of the Palace was bent as a nine-bob note and HIV Positive. Chris, Shelley's ex-boyfriend, was Mrs Dillon's dope delivery boy. Helen had slept with Sammy's art teacher three times. Colin had a dirty magazine hidden under his comics.

He sat in the darkened room, in his seat at the head of the table. He felt as if he were the dark heart of the town. He could see the glowing lines that connected everything. He knew everything there was to be known. But he still couldn't remember the child who'd grown up to be a writer.

Shelley was leaving for East Anglia. He gave her an envelope full of £50 notes to supplement her grant. She was the only one he had any time for. He hoped Sammy would grow up to be like Shelley, but there was not much chance of that now, the kids being with their mother, raised to be mini-Helens.

'Good-bye, monster,' Shelley said, kissing his cold cheek.

She walked away, her long, black coat outlining her sleek figure. She reminded Hackwill of the actress who played the Devil in the *Where the Bodies Are Buried* films. Before she was out of sight, she turned and gave him an encouraging wave.

The bulldozers were still there, under tarpaulins. Work was supposed to resume any day, as soon as the surviving McKinnell Brothers had sorted out their complicated tangle of affairs. Ben McKinnell had been heavily insured and the cash injection would keep the Development going. Hackwill thought it would never be finished: the Development would drag on forever, spreading across Denbeigh Gardens to swamp the close where Mrs Dillon lived, then sprawling through the town, ripping up the roads and parks and houses, replacing asphalt with mud.

He stood where the Gardens had been, soil clogging the soles of his shoes. Holes were excavated all around like mass graves. He'd been spending a lot of time here, loitering, thinking. He walked carefully across the bare earth. It was dark and the ground was treacherous.

There was a bright moon to guide him, but he knew where the chasms were anyway. This was his country, for he was a monster. That was something he accepted. He had scraped bare this scar on the town map. Everything that got in his way, he had removed.

He wondered when he'd he become a monster. When he saw the poster for *Where the Bodies Are Buried* in Valerie's Video? When Allan Keyes first turned on his word processor and dredged up a name from his own past for a made-up character? When he had accepted his first consultancy fee? Or back in the playground, when Reg and he had picked out a solitary little boy and made a mark on his mind?

'It was here,' a voice said.

Reg stood by the bulldozer, wrapped up warm in an anorak. Hackwill had noticed him hanging around on the fringes of his one-eyed vision for days now.

'We used to play here, remember?'

Hackwill realised it was true. Ash Grove, closed down years ago, was a few streets away. Denbeigh Gardens had been on the way to and from school.

'Allan used to make up stories about a monster in the shed,' he said, remembering at last. 'It ate eyes.'

'Found his vocation,' Reg said. 'If you hadn't made him drink loo-water, he wouldn't be in Beverly Hills porking popsies in bikinis and shovelling half Colombia up his nose.'

Hackwill remembered the screwed-up child-face, leaking tears. The face was close, because he was holding the kid's shoulders, shaking them. Reg egged him on, making suggestions, darting about like an ape, grinning and laughing.

'The little shit *owes* you, Robbo,' Reg said.

Hackwill found a pick-axe in his hands. It had been stuck into a pile of rubble like the sword in the stone. His long-nailed fingers gripped the wooden handle.

'He shouldn't have done what he did, made you a laughing-stock.'

'Allan didn't mean anything, Reg,' Hackwill said, swinging. 'Rob Hackwill just came to life and got away from him.'

Allan Keyes had picked the wrong name for his playground demon. Like everybody, he hadn't remembered properly. Hackwill would never have chosen Allan if it hadn't been for Reg. Yet again, he'd let Hackwill take the consequences.

The pick-point sank into Reg's breast-bone and came out from between his back-ribs. The Independent emptied his lungs in a reverse gulp and blood burst from his mouth. Hackwill pulled the implement free and Reg tottered.

He growled, 'Get the point?'

Reg extended his arms as black blood squirted from his mouth and the hole in his chest. Every time he'd ever been in trouble, Reg had been there, guilty and chuckling and safe. Hackwill reached out a claw-hand and took a patch out of the Independent's face. He crumpled it in his fist like a slimy leaf, then dropped it.

'What's the matter,' he snarled, wiping his hand on Reg's anorak, 'why the fallen face?'

It wasn't fair, but he had to accept it: he was Rob Hackwill, the monster.

Reg stood at the lip of one of the excavations. With a prodding finger, Hackwill toppled him backwards. The grave-darkness swallowed him.

Hackwill looked up at the night sky and laughed, a red film on his vision turning the moon into a blood-eye. As far as anyone was concerned, he was *the* Rob Hackwill.

He stood on the brink, kicking in earth on top of the dead man. Reg's white and red face disappeared under black clods.

Looking up from the hole, a gust of wind hit his frozen face. His shut eye shocked open and he saw figures where the swings had been. A small child on the ground; another, bigger one on top of him, holding his face into earth; and one standing by, looking out for adults, chuckling.

The wind passed and his eye closed again, shutting out the children. His face was set. He saw only the place that was his home now, a playground turned to a graveyard. Rob Hackwill squatted in the shadows between piles of earth, a night-creature hiding from the dawn.

WHERE THE BODIES ARE BURIED II:
SEQUEL HOOK

The deal was on the table and, though his American agent told him he was insane, Allan Keyes was going to take it.

It's not like you're signing your soul away for nothing, the voice said silently, *you have a percentage of the gross.*

Ray Calme, President of New Frontier Pictures, had the script in one hand, the contract in the other. The contract was thicker than the script and word-processed to a higher standard. According to Whit Pulsford, Allan's agent, it was also more frightening.

Where the Bodies Are Buried would be *An Allan Keyes Film.*

'Allan,' Calme said, 'I like you. I like you oh so much. We're going to make pots o' money.'

What do you mean 'we', kimosabe?

Allan shifted in his chrome and leather s-m chair while Calme weighed the documents as if he were a Scale of Justice. New Frontier, despite the Hollywood address, wasn't a studio but a suite of offices above a loan company. They rented facilities on a film-by-film basis and were strictly non-union.

'You Brits, you're like visionaries. Look at Alan Parker, Adrian Lyne...'

Neither of whom have ever made a film that was any good, actually.

'Tony Scott, Roland Joffé!'

Good grief.

'And Renaissance men! To have a real, live novelist who can also direct a film...'

That's a moot point...

'Forget *Karnage*,' Calme said, 'it's in the used-tapes-from-$2.99 bin. The theatrical prints are guitar plectrums.'

Allan was uncomfortable. After all this sweet talk, he expected to get royally screwed.

'This is a chance for you to start over.'

Last year, Allan had made it into the Top Ten of *Film Threat*'s 'Frigid Fifty', a list of the people least likely to get another job in Hollywood not involving parking cars or asking 'still or sparkling?' all day. Having seen most of *Karnage*, the film with his name on it, Allan thought the magazine overestimated his career prospects.

'*Where the Bodies Are Buried*, is going to change industry perception of you,' Calme continued, happily lining up script and contract on his teakwood desk. 'And it'll get New Frontier some respect. Trust me.'

The air conditioner buzzed like a meat-grinder, reminding Allan of New Frontier movies: *Hacksaw Hookers*, *The Cincinnati Flamethrower Holocaust*, *Gross*. Surprisingly few were in-house productions. Calme preferred to pick up cheapies made in Europe or by semi-amateurs in Nowhere America, splice in tits 'n' gore, and slap on a high concept title. Calme had titles in his drawer he'd not yet been able to find films to fit. They had first met when Calme tried to buy up *Chitinous Splinters*, his student film, and rename it *Bug Bomb*.

'This monster, this Rob Hackwill, he's gonna be like Frankenstein for the eighties, for the *nineties*. Just from reading the script and looking at the sketches the make-up goons have worked up, I can't sleep for thinking about the son-of-a-bitch.'

Calme made a snarly monster face and claw-gestured, impersonating Rob Hackwill.

Maybe you should play the part, Ray-Ban.

'It's a dynamite scary idea, Allan. The blackmailer who knows everything and can't be killed. The monster who knows where the bodies are buried and won't ever let up.'

un film de Allan Keyes ... for best achievement in direction, the nominees are...

'By the time New Frontier does the sequel, we won't be able to afford you.'

'There can't be a sequel,' Allan said, quietly. 'At the end, I'm killing him forever. It's part of the ritual.'

'You'll be at Pyramid or Warners, making *mucho dinero*,' Calme said, rubbing his thumb against his fingers. 'You know who used to get coffee for me?'

Roger Rabbit?

'Oliver Stone. Now he won't talk to me in the street. I can't get him on the phone. Next year, that's you.'

This year, this month, this day, Allan Keyes had precisely one American screen credit. That was only because his deal had been worded so he couldn't take his name off *Karnage*. His directorial career consisted of *Chitinous Splinters*, a piece of student surrealism that sometimes turned up after midnight on public television, the werewolf episodes of *Emmerdale Farm*, and two weeks fighting to preserve his script for *Karnage*, only to find himself unceremonially booted off set in favour of his producer's college room-mate. In interviews, the *Karnage* krewe claimed he was a dilettante who didn't know how to take a lens cap off. Ray Calme was his only chance to become an official director. A *writer*-director.

'You and Ollie,' Calme said, letting one hand savagely attack the other. 'Like this.'

The deal was that Calme would let Allan make *Where the Bodies Are Buried* in return for a fifth of the fee even New Frontier would pay for the script if a writer weren't attached to it as director.

The crazy thing was that Allan, alone in a city of table-waiting Hitchcocks and valet-parking Antonionis, didn't *want* to be a director. He had always been more interested in prose, and had gone to film school almost on a whim. The *Emmerdale* assignment, coming in the middle of a decade of scribbling underemployment, had been a surprise and an ordeal, crawling along because someone somewhere had happy memories of how stoned he was during the brief festival run of *Chitinous Splinters*.

Allan didn't even want to be in the Big Parking Lot of Lo-Cal, USA. Like Lesley, his long-term live-in, he *preferred* the British climate. He had constant twinges that he should get back to Somerset and just be a writer. But the movie thing bit deep: after watching *Karnage* aborted under other hands, what he wanted was to protect his baby.

It's the world's most powerful natural instinct, after all.

Calme, smiling his professorial drug dealer's smile, patted the script gently, and hugged the contract (his baby) to the *Hacksaw Hookers* T-shirt he wore under a Savile Row suitcoat. Allan had been surprised to learn, from a New Frontier hand-out, that Ray Calme had a degree in industrial chemistry.

'Theatre owners are going to hate you, Allan, because *Bodies* is going to make people shit with fright. No kidding, they'll have to replace seat-covers every performance.'

Allan knew that, compared with Ray Calme, the idiot who mutilated *Karnage* was liable to have his life's work preserved by the Museum of Modern Art. The New Frontier formula was 95% tits 'n' gore, plus 5% crappy jokes. Allan, still deep down the underage horror fan who had sneaked into the Palace to see the X-certificated *Devil Daughter of Dracula*, had never been able to get to the end of a New Frontier movie without pain.

'Allan,' Calme said, 'I know we can do real business.'

The step was taken and he was committed, for better or flamethrower holocaust. Allan relaxed.

'I have notes,' Calme said, indicating the script.

Allan was prepared to be reasonable, to take advice on board and weigh it up, then shoot what he wanted anyway.

Most of the agony was in the past. When reworking 'A Trickle of Shame' as a screenplay, Allan had switched the story's West Country setting into an American Mid-West that owed more to movies than experience. The middle-aged teacher heroine became a teenage high-schooler and the dead serious monster grew a nastily twisted sense of humour. Still, the heart of the piece was untouched; the story retained its integrity, its subtext. There was a seriously scary point to it all.

'I love the scene where the bimbo's boobs come to life and slap her around,' Calme said, chuckling. 'Don't change a word of the script.'

Except, he means, to limit the action to as few sets as possible to save on carpentry.

Allan had been trying to wrap personal concerns in a commercial package. He was, so far, pleased to come up with something which appealed to Ray Calme but wouldn't disappoint his readers. In the end, he was doing this deal because he couldn't stand to go to another convention and have to explain how other people had turned a perfectly-formed story like *Karnage* into celluloid sludge.

Calme leafed through the script, amusing himself.

'The guy's tongue exploding his head? Outstanding.'

The effect would cost more than the actor. But it would be worth it.

Calme came to the end.

'Here's my problem,' he said.

Allan's heart froze.

'After the monster is torn apart by the ghosts of his victims, you have

Tina, the tits girl, shut the scrapbook on him, and there's a flaming "End" title?'

Allan nodded. That was how he saw *Where the Bodies Are Buried* finishing.

'It's like the Hammer Films,' Allan explained. 'You leave with the dust of Dracula blowing in the wind. I'm fed up with the non-endings films have these days. It's all over and then you see there's one monster still under the floorboards. It cheats the audience.'

'Yeah, yeah, good stuff, Allan, right enough. But, for $15,000 and a shot at director, you've got to give me a sequel hook.'

At one o'clock in the morning, Allan got home to the rented house he had left twenty hours earlier. The first day of shooting was done, and he wanted to shove his head through a plate-glass door.

Lesley had stayed up, and made Ovaltine and sandwiches for him as he sat in the cramped kitchen and wound down. They had been together for so long he didn't even need to tell her what he wanted in his sandwiches. She didn't ask him what it had been like.

His nerves were still singing. He could still hear the clatter and chatter of the set.

'I don't know,' he said.

Heh heh heh...

'Maybe there's a way this can work...'

Lesley put an arm around him and helped him to bed.

Two middle-aged couples walked out in the first fifteen minutes, shaking their heads and complaining about the noise. A blast of Heavy Metal followed them from the auditorium. Calme said that was good; he'd be ashamed to make a horror film parents liked.

Suddenly, it's Ray-Ban who 'makes' the films, isn't it?

Before anyone outside an edit suite had seen an assembly of *Where the Bodies Are Buried*, Allan had signed, for over five times the money, to direct *City Hammer*, an action script by a British comics creator. He knew he'd have to rewrite, without credit. Not as personal a project as his own film, it would show he could explode a helicopter with the best of them. It was a step out of the gutter, away from New Frontier; not to a Major, but to a high-profile Independent, Mojacar. Also, as Whit told him, it got him taken seriously. In this town, people judged worth by asking price. It was better to have directed a schlocky flop for $80,000 than a sleeper hit for $15,000. It was especially useful, Whit now conceded, to have leaped from $15,000 to $80,000; that curve should land Allan $400,000 for his first studio project (probably a big budget sequel) and, if that hit, settle him in the $2,000,000 club until he had a monster that edged in with the Spielbergs and John Hugheses in the *Variety* Top Ten Grossers, whereupon his asking price entered the Twilight Zone.

Getting ahead of ourselves, aren't we?

Calme had driven Allan, and a couple of New Frontier suits who hadn't showed their faces during the actual shooting, out to Westwood for a sneak preview of *Where the Bodies Are Buried*. Lesley, who'd lived with the traumas of creation but never seen footage, had gone inside to find out what the agony was about, but Allan, along with the New Frontier brass, kept to the foyer.

A scattering of cast and crew also turned up, including Mal Gariazzo, the tinily energetic Italian-American who seemed possessed by the wicked spirit of Rob Hackwill. His screen time was limited and he was billed eleventh but his snakily crazed performance would elevate him from 'who is... ?' to 'get me... !' Before landing the part, for which he'd campaigned intensively, he'd been in New Frontier beach bimbo films as the hero's geeky friend who didn't get laid and threw up on the wet T-shirt queen. Now he'd be up for the British villain's sadistic sidekick in action blockbusters.

As the film unspooled, Gariazzo, in a much-strapped leather jump-suit, nervously stalked the foyer, chain-munching popcorn. Without the glowing red eye, mangled face, exposed teeth and steel claws, he was unrecognisable as the monster, but occasionally he gave out horribly unmistakable Rob Hackwill laughs.

Mal-de-merde thinks he's Rob Hackwill, does he?

Where the Bodies Are Buried was being shown after a Christian Slater film; the theatre was packed with teenage couples and gaggles of girls. From the foyer, Allan could tell exactly where the movie was by the pitch of the screams. He knew the film to the shot, to the *second*, and he could feel in his stomach an excitement that corresponded with the crescendos of tension and the pay-offs of shock.

'It's the tongue next,' he said.

He could have sworn the auditorium doors swelled outwards with the rush of audible fear. Then came a ripple of relieved laughter and a settling-down as the scene changed.

Gariazzo chortled and clawed the air in triumph. He took his power personally. The monster's crazy-funny streak came directly from the actor. Allan couldn't help but look at Gariazzo sometimes as if he were his daughter's first boyfriend.

Remember, you signed the paper, Daddy. You don't own Rob Hackwill. New Frontier does.

After about an hour, during the flashback when Hackwill was taken to Hell and given his mission of vengeance by the Devil Princess, a girl in her early teens was helped out of the cinema by a clutch of her friends. She was sobbing silently and unsteady on her ankles.

'We should get a pub shot of that,' Calme chortled.

'Wow,' said one of the girls, '*intense!*'

'Can I get the door for you?' Gariazzo asked, a Hackwill croak in his voice.

The hysterical teenager looked at the innocently-smiling actor and went cross-eyed as she fainted. Gariazzo laughed his normal laugh. Calme was suddenly concerned, thinking of lawsuits. The audience screamed again. Allan Keyes had arrived.

'As adults, we forget the wonders and terrors of childhood,' Allan told Turner Mockridge, the withered kid from *Fangoria*. 'Children are permanently afraid. Me, I was besieged by this vast, formless, black wall of fear. It's the flipside of the magic and it lasts longer. You remember Wicked Witches better than Munchkins. With *Bodies*, I wanted to come to grips with the fear, to bring it back with an adult subtext. Let's face it, you no longer have to worry about a bigger kid snatching your dinner money, but as you grow up the world gets more complicated. It was bad enough being afraid of losing your school custard, now you have to be afraid of losing your house, your job, your marriage. Scary, isn't it?'

Yes.

The boyish, balding genre journalist looked at his digital notepad. He was the only badly dressed person Allan had met in California.

'Where did *Where the Bodies Are Buried* come from?'

'A diseased little tumour inside my brain. Actually, I was thinking about the EC Philosophy of Cosmic Justice. You know the EC horror comics of the fifties?'

Mockridge nodded an 'of course'. Asking the Man From *Fango* that was like asking a literature professor if he knew D.H. Lawrence.

'Most of their stories follow a simple format. It certainly wasn't original to William M. Gaines. Since *The Haunt of Fear* was before my time, I came to know the formula through the Amicus films of the early seventies. It was also common in *The Pan Book of Horror Stories*, not that a heathen American would know what that was, and *The Twilight Zone*. Essentially, you have a protagonist who goes around being a complete bastard until God drops a brick on his head. The subtext is that people who bring evil into the world but are beyond human law invoke a cosmic justice that allows for a horribly ironic fate.'

'Like the vivisectionist who is kidnapped by aliens and experimented on?'

'That was a famous one. Robert Bloch always used Cosmic Justice as an excuse for a bitter pun. You know, "cat got your tongue"?'

'You used the format in *Strange Segments*. In 'Off-Ground Touch', for instance, where the middle-aged guy goes back to the school where he was a bully and gets menaced by the adult-sized children. Isn't it limiting for a full-length film?'

'It would be. It's basically a lazy man's short story outline. What I've tried to do in *Where the Bodies Are Buried* is examine the metaphysical workings that would allow for that kind of plot. Rob Hackwill, as we learn in the flashback, was a typical EC protagonist, a scumbag blackmailer who was tortured, mutilated and murdered by his victims and buried by dead of night in the town graveyard. His punishment in the afterlife is to become the wholesale implement of Cosmic Justice. The Devil Princess, my version of the ruler of a malign but ordered universe, sends him back as a monster vigilante. Everybody in town was rotten in the first place, or Hackwill wouldn't have been able to blackmail them. He merely ups the stakes by forgetting money and extorting pain, fear and, ahem, hideous physical transformations.'

'Your work always comes down to a sense of order and justice?'

'That's a very astute insight, Turner. Indeed, Hackwill is all-powerful until he comes up against a truly innocent person, our heroine.'

Mockridge thought it over for a moment, digesting what had been said.

Allan, always delighted to dissect his own work, wondered if he had given away too many plot points.

'Now the question I am obliged by law to ask. What will your next film project be? Will it be horror?'

'*City Hammer* is science fiction action but it'll have monsters in it. I'm already perverting it in the rewrite. When I see an opening to scare people, I can't resist shouting "boo"!'

'Do you plan on continuing in the genre, as a writer and as a film-maker?'

'I can't see anywhere else to go. Writing about middle-class women who get cancer doesn't really appeal to me. I'd have the cancer be a living, thinking thing. Thus far, I've not had an idea which would take me beyond the boundaries of the genre continent into that cold clime they call the mainstream. I'm not one of those who'll say, you know, "this picture may be called *Werewolf Cheerleaders*, but it's not a horror movie, it's about relationships". I'd like it on the record that *Where the Bodies Are Buried* is a fuck of a horror film and I'd really like it to terrify people.'

By the premiere, Allan decided he could bear to watch *Where the Bodies Are Buried* again.

Sensing a chance for the kind of acclaim *Hacksaw Hookers* never had a hope of, Ray Calme had arranged a midnight matinee for celebrities from the world of horror. At first, response was disappointing: genre professionals had seen too many New Frontier pictures on tape to risk venturing out to the Century Pantheon to catch another *Cincinnati Flamethrower Holocaust* on the big screen. Allan's rep as a writer helped: the short story collection *Strange Segments*, while not the hot book it had been in England, had been well-received in America, and the novel *Busting a Gut* (which Stephen King said turned his hair white) brushed the lower end of the *New York Times* Best-Seller list. He had been profiled by *Cinefantastique*. Word was out that, as films directed by writers go, *Where the Bodies Are Buried* was more like *Hellraiser* than *Maximum Overdrive*.

A lot more like Hellraiser, *eh, Mr Plagiarist? All those dangling chains...*

Mal Gariazzo, in full Hackwill drag, escorted Breeze Brasselle, the 'scream queen' who played the Devil Princess. They camped it up outside the Pantheon, posing with embarrassed guests as a phalanx of photographers snapped like turtles. Forrest J Ackerman, Joe Bob Briggs and Elvira got into the spirit. Dennis Etchison looked as if he'd rather be somewhere else. Calme checked the guest-list: Alice Cooper, John Carpenter and David Schow had arrived; David Cronenberg, Ray Bradbury and Barbara Steele were no-shows so far. Mimes dressed as monsters mingled with the guests, offering trays of scary canapés: sugar tarantulas and sausage slugs.

A few people asked Lesley who she was and skittered away when she nodded at Allan and said 'I'm with the band'. Her only comment after the preview had been 'well, you can still surprise me.' The first time Whit had met Lesley, he'd told her she would have to watch Allan around all the starlets. Then, she had said she could handle it – her Deputy Head pay had supported them through years of his unsteady writing income – but now she might have changed her mind.

Breeze stuck her tongue down Allan's throat for the photographers. Lesley looked up at the sky and shook her head the way Allan's mother used to.

City Hammer was in the can after four nightmare weeks in the desert with stunt-drivers and radioactive mutants, and Whit had meetings set up at Pyramid and Universal. The galleys of *Cornworld* were out at the studios, and the rights bidding started at $250,000. It was written into any deal that Allan would script and direct the film. An expansive fantasy with a New Age twist, *Cornworld* could very well be the Next Big Thing. He'd come a long way from St Louis. Sedgmoor, rather.

My-my, high muckety-muck, Mr Keyes. Next you'll be forgetting who got you where you are.

A nasty wind blew through the plaza outside the Pantheon, lifting the webby skirts of women at the *première* discarded wrappers across the forecourt like crippled insects. This development was supposed to be litter-free, but – like the street people the Pantheon employed uniformed security men to exclude – rubbish had a way of creeping back in.

In the lobby, Allan sipped his New Frontier wine (ten cents a gallon, unless he misjudged Calme) and noticed how people he knew quite well avoided talking to him. After the film, that would be different, he hoped. It took a lot to scare professionals but he thought he had more than a lot.

It's just a question of knowing their secrets. That's what scares people, Allan. Knowing, heh heh heh, Where the Bodies Are Buried.

Everyone filed into the auditorium at midnight. Allan and Lesley took their reserved seats in the back row, and Lesley patted him on the arm, forgiving him for the Scream Queen. Calme, who loved to strut about in public and take credit, made a speech which was greeted with sceptical laughter. Then the film played.

By the finale, Allan was in love with his baby again. Months of post-production tinkering had made him hate *Where the Bodies Are Buried*. As the soundtrack was laid in (he wanted a harpsichord concerto, Calme insisted on a 'hot band' named Putrid) and the effects scenes were optically enhanced (why hadn't that eyeball burst on cue?), he'd become intensely aware of the film's deformities. The sets looked cheap, the acting was variable at best, the exposition came in an unwieldy lump near the end, Hackwill should never have come out of the shadows and the good shots reminded him of other, better films.

Isaac, the veteran editor, had helped with the delivery and made sure the child's head was on the right way round. Cynthia Vanning, the 28-year-old teenage heroine, had only three facial expressions; but Isaac, who had valuable experience on Lassie movies, manipulated off-cuts of film to jerk her strings to such an extent that she actually seemed to be giving a performance.

Even this audience reacted. They were scared.

Got them.

It wasn't 'A Trickle of Shame', but it was a film. With less money and fewer resources, he had done better than *Karnage*. On that alone, he could retire with dignity and write for the rest of his days.

Deep down, he liked it a little less than *Chitinous Splinters*.

Lesley's hand was around his upper arm, fingers biting like little snakes. He could feel her cringe at every superbly-orchestrated shock. Even second time through, it worked.

Rob Hackwill was dragged back to Hell and his victims tore him apart. Gobbets of fire were slung around. Gariazzo even managed to work a little sympathy in for the monster. In the end, like Kong and Karloff's Monster, he was a victim too.

One big scream and the ashes settled. Then came the scene Allan had never been able to love. He had written it, had filmed it, but could never *feel* it. After the end of Allan Keyes's *Where the Bodies Are Buried*, came the Ray Calme scene, the sequel hook.

It was all over but it was starting again. Tina, having survived, was in the school bathrooms, smoking and remembering. The faces of all her dead friends drifted by in the mirror.

Not a bad effect, he conceded, grudgingly.

Then came that godawful Heavy Metal and the monster exploded out of a toilet bowl, red-eyed and cackling. Everyone jumped and the Putrid music crashed over the credits.

The buzz was incredible. People who had avoided him all evening congratulated him. Whit had his pocket calculator out and estimated the opening weekend gross. Gariazzo took bows and did the laugh. Mockridge told Lesley he expected a sweep of the Chainsaw Awards. Calme puffed a cigar as if he were David O. Selznick the night *Gone With the Wind* came home with Oscar. Clive Barker didn't mention the familiar dangling chains.

Only Allan noticed the sequel hook. And his constant companion.

That ending, Allan. It's shit. It was a bad mistake. It'll come back to haunt you.

'... not since *Elm Street One* ... *Carrie* ... *Chain Saw* ... *Psycho* ...'

And if it doesn't, I *will.*

Cornworld was in turnaround for a rewrite (Pyramid wanted it bigger, plus the Green Man role written larger for Sean Connery) and *Pixie Patrol*, outlined well before *Where the Bodies Are Buried* and nearly forgotten, was suddenly a 'go' project. Pyramid said it was a good move to do a medium-budget studio film before taking on the Herculean labour of *Cornworld*.

His writer-director fee on *Pixie Patrol* was close to the entire below-the-line budget of *Where the Bodies Are Buried*. The script was about a streetwise black cop, played by comedian Muldoon Pezz, partnered with an elfin warrior to reclaim Excalibur from a power-crazed televangelist played, with the most British accent imaginable, by Julian Sands. Mal Gariazzo was pencilled in for the villain's sadistic sidekick, a heart-eating troll passing for human. For five minutes, it looked as if Allan would have to rewrite the lead for Whoopi Goldberg, then Pezz, needing a family hit to offset his drugs bust, committed. The deal fell in place overnight and shooting was due to start in three days.

Allan was by his pool, getting a massage, when Amaranth, his assistant, brought out a phone and asked him if he would take a call from Ray Calme. New Frontier had been trying to get to him all week, and he knew he would have to talk eventually.

He hadn't seen his old producer since *Where the Bodies Are Buried* pipped $40,000,000 in domestic box office. In a follow-up interview with Mockridge, Allan moaned about studio-imposed bad music and the cop-out ending. Calme sent *Fangoria* a letter about how artists didn't understand the real business of making movies.

'Allan, doll, how are you?' the tiny voice buzzed.

'Fine, Ray.'

'I saw *City Hammer*. Good picture.'

'That's one way of putting it.'

There are good things in it, Allan. They're just spaced pretty evenly among the crap things.

Allan gripped the phone tightly and the masseuse ran up against some knots.

'How are things at the Majors? See Oliver Stone much?'

Expert hands worked the aches around his neck. Sunlight shimmered on the waters of the pool. Prescription designer shades cut out the glare.

'Did you glom this week's *Hollywood Reporter*?'

'Yes.'

'What do you think?'

New Frontier had taken out a full-page ad, announcing 'Ray (*Hacksaw Hookers*) Calme Presents ... Mal (Rob Hackwill!!!) Gariazzo in ... Allan Keyes's *Where the Bodies Are Buried, Part II: Hackwill's Back!* (Credits Not Contractual).'

'I'd have changed a couple of words if you'd run it by me.'

'Which words?'

'"Allan Keyes's".'

'It's in your contract. Anything made from the *Bodies* premise, which New Frontier *owns*, has to be "An Allan Keyes Film". It's a good deal for you. You get your $15,000 all over again for *nada*.'

You made $15,000 before breakfast this morning. Once you get out here by the pool, money creeps in on autopilot.

'This Hackwill thing is big, Allan.'

The monster – *Allan's* monster – was being merchandised extensively by New Frontier. A *Where the Bodies Are Buried* comic book was forthcoming from Dark Horse and the Gore Store was marketing a Hackwill mask for Halloween. Every movie and monster magazine had done multiple covers with Gariazzo-as-Hackwill leering, looming, clutching, goggling or drooling. Allan's creation had become the Princess Di of the bizarro generation. Whit, soon to be Allan's former agent, hadn't negotiated a cut of any spin-off rights, though he had tied in compensations to the sequel clause.

'It's getting out of hand. I've had to take on an extra girl to handle all the Hackwill requests. Joe Bob has made him "Beast of the Year". Mal is doing the *Tonight Show* in character.'

Allan, of course, had followed his wayward child's progress. The less scary Hackwill got, the less interested Allan was in him.

You're a bad parent. You should love me, however I turn out.

'I know we can't afford you to direct,' Calme said, 'we've got a line on the chick who did the Putrid videos.'

'Ellen Jeanette Sheridan?'

'That's her. Great talent. Like Walter Hill and Barbara Streisand in one package. She's hungry for a shot. She's comfortable with rubber. She's done a script.'

She's done a script?

'You'll love it. It's close to the first one. Mal's got more to do. It's more up-front about Hackwill. After all, he's who the kids pay to see. Frankenstein for the nineties. We've licensed the hobby kit.'

A cloud-shadow flitted over the sun, letting a wedge of cold fall briefly. Allan shivered and the masseuse soothed his gooseflesh away. His new $500 haircut itched.

'I'd like to work out an arrangement on *Bodies II*, Allan. If you'd just look at the script. Pencil out a few lines, scribble in a gag or two, dot some Ts and cross some Is.'

'I start shooting next week.'

'Yeah, yeah. Really, you don't have to read Ellen Jeanette's script. Just approve it. You'll get co-story credit, $50,000 loose cash, and a per cent of the gross. All for not doing anything.'

They'll make it any way, whatever you do. They have the right. You gave me away, Dad. You sold me into slavery for a lousy fifteen grand. Forever.

'I really don't have time.'

'Allan, just do some pub when the film goes theatrical. We want you on board. You are the genius, the creator, the originator. Ellen Jeanette is in awe of you. Believe me, if you want a fast blow job at New Frontier, this girl is for you. She doesn't want to violate your vision. She sees herself as the channel through which you can work.'

You made me alone, master. Make me a bride, or I shall be with you on your wedding night...

'Shut yer neck,' Allan muttered.

'What was that?'

'Nothing, Ray. Look, I'll take it under advisement.'

'Just give us your blessing, just wish us well'

'Ray, make the film you want.'

The call was over.

I'm melting, meltiiiiing. They'll torture me, Dad. They'll do things you can't imagine. They're *the monsters, them, them, them.*

'So,' Mockridge asked, '*Pixie Patrol*, eh? That's doesn't sound like the Allan Keyes who gave us *Busting a Gut* and Rob Hackwill?'

'Wait until you've seen the movie, Turner,' Allan replied, 'I think you'll be surprised. I'm trying for a hard-edged fantasy. PG-13 sure, but we'll expand the ratings envelope. With a big sword macguffin, the temptation was to lop off heads and I've never been one to resist temptation.'

'But is it *horror*?'

'I think *Fango* won't be disappointed. Mal Gariazzo is aboard, eating some interesting new things.'

'What about the *Bodies* sequel? Are you involved?'

'I take a remote, paternal interest. But children have to leave home some time. I hope Rob Hackwill is in good hands, because if mistreated he has a way of settling accounts that can be, as they say, final.'

'Allan,' Lesley said, 'this is nothing to do with you, but there's nothing for me here.'

She wasn't qualified to work in the US school system, and even if she started jumping through the hoops it would be decades before she could reach her former position.

West Somerset College said they would keep her Deputy Head-ship open for only six months and time was almost up.

'I have enough money for us both,' Allan said. 'Really, neither of us ever need to work again.'

'It's not about money either.' Lesley shrugged, unable to explain. 'It's a quality of life decision.'

*

One thing about being where he was; he never *ever* had to be alone. Allan made Lesley a gift of their old flat, paying off the mortgage with option money on a four-page story. After years of unwedded cohabitation, he'd been enjoying his bachelorhood. He specialised in the sort of girls who would have ignored him as a geeky teenager and who grew in clumps around the swimming pools out here.

Life was hectic. Going to a restaurant was a major operation, like invading France. At horror conventions, he was a top-of-the-bill guest. He turned down three-quarters of the TV and print interview requests.

Horror? No, I wouldn't really say I write horror. I'm a metaphysical romancer...

With *Cornworld* a Number One Best-Seller, he was an A-list Hollywood invitee; a *novelist* who could talk movies. Everyone he met had read the coverage, a few had even tried the book. In this town, he was glamorously intellectual, but he could play the game. When numbers were crunched, *Where the Bodies Are Buried* had a better cost-to-profit ratio than any major studio release of the last two years.

His new agency were pushing heavy for the *Cornworld* movie. It could be next summer's biggie. *Pixie Patrol* was nothing to be ashamed of, even if it faded after three weeks. After an opening weekend splash, it failed to grow legs.

He got back to the house and circumvented security. He dumped his keys in the tray on the hall-table. The place sounded empty which, after the noise of the evening, was what he wanted. Sometimes, it was blissful to be where nobody could hear you scream. By the tray was a package and a note from Amaranth.

He opened the package and found a cassette. It was an advance cut of *Where the Bodies Are Buried, Part II* with a scribbled compliments slip from Ray Calme. 'Ellen Jeanette is dying to know what you think.' Ellen Jeanette was well under five feet tall, had white hair down to her calves and suffered permanent hearing impairment from working with too many loud rock bands.

Busy on *Pixie Patrol*, even taking a trip back to Britain to do promotion and see Lesley installed in the West Country, he'd not kept up with *Hackwill's Back!* He'd read the script until the voice in his head yelled so loud he couldn't turn the pages and had reasoned that the whole thing had nothing to do with him.

Abandoner, betrayer, ravager!

Apart from the alcoholic police captain, the nymphomaniac French teacher and the perverted school janitor – and Hackwill, if he counted – all the characters in Ellen Jeanette Sheridan's screenplay were under eighteen. Allan thought the sequel would turn out like *Grange Hill* with tits 'n' gore. No, make that *Beverly Hills 90210* with tits 'n' gore. Back in Britain, with an 18 rating, nobody who would want to see *Hackwill's Back!* would legally be able to.

He might as well watch the thing now. If he fell asleep, he could always have the ending with his cornflakes tomorrow.

After making himself an Ovaltine in the bunker-like kitchen, he fired up the wall-sized projection video. Before settling down, he saluted the eighteen-inch Screamin' Rob Hackwill kit posed by the screen. Then he sprawled on the newly-installed, personalised divan, and tucked his legs under him. This was how he remembered watching Patrick Troughton as *Doctor Who* in the sixties, when he was just learning the business of frightening people.

His parents had encouraged his interest in monsters, because somehow it made him less frightened. As a child, his problem had been nightmares. Often, he'd been kept back from school, which had its own horrors, through lack of sleep. The day he glued together his first glow-in-the-dark Aurora monster (the Wolf Man, pumped-up plastic torso considerably more muscular than the one sported by a hairy Lon Chaney Jr in the film) the nightmares stopped. If there were monsters, then there were monster-destroyers and the universe purged itself of evil, at least until the sequel. Since then, he hadn't been afraid. At school even, the horrors went away. When he started telling stories about monsters, the other kids – one of whom *had* been called Hackwill – stopped hitting and started listening. He had discovered his power.

Where is Robert Hackwill of Ash Grove Primary these days? Do you suppose he's seen your little film?

He zapped the remote. The screen was black. He sipped Ovaltine. Red slashes appeared, making up a stylised Rob face. Then the title, in letters of fire. *Where the Bodies Are Buried, Part II: Hackwill's Back!*. Gariazzo-as-Hackwill exploded snarling through the title, lipless teeth chattering, red eye burning.

There was no story in the first ten minutes, just images. Putrid struck power chords and pretty pictures stumbled over the screen as if Ellen Jeanette had forgotten not to make another rock video. So far as Allan could understand, Hackwill was crawling back from Hell, reassembling himself.

The film cut out and the screen became a black mirror. Allan saw himself huddled, cooling cup in his hands, goggling at the nothing.

All this expensive equipment, and it still doesn't work.

The image moved, as if the camera were circling. It panned steadily, until it was no longer a reflection, but a view from behind the divan. The screen showed the back of Allan's head as he looked at a screen which showed the back of Allan's head as he looked at a screen which showed the back of Allan's head... Smaller and smaller screen images zoomed to an infinite distance which tugged at him, threatening to pull the real Allan into the screen to fall forever into the vortex.

He turned, but there was no camera behind him. Just the framed original Carson artwork for the *Cornworld* cover.

On screen, Allan was distracted by a sound. Ovaltine spilled as he jumped. A nanosecond later, unnerved by the fissure between real and reflected, Allan spilled his own drink. Warm stickiness spread across his thighs.

The film Allan got up and Ellen Jeanette cut to a close-up. Allan's heart began beating again. The man in the film wasn't his reflection, but an actor playing a character who happened to be dressed like him and in a set which was almost, but not quite, identical to the room he was sitting in. The actor, football player shoulders straining his jacket, didn't even look much like him.

Could this be some silly in-joke?

The actor made frightened faces as something scratched at the window. Allan couldn't remember any of this in the script. He couldn't help darting a look at his own unscratched windows. Outside, everything was dark. As he turned his head, the film showed a view of its windows. The shape of Hackwill was out there, unmistakable. The single red eye glowed.

'*I know everything, Kiss,*' Hackwill snarled, nastily. '*About the girls, the parties, the pay-offs, the drugs...*'

The character – Kiss? – was horrorstruck.

As *Hackwill's Back!* played on, Allan got angry. The high school story had been junked and the rewrite substituted a frankly libellous plot about a writer named, transparently, Adam Kiss. Instrumental in the original death of the blackmailer from Hell, Adam got rich on a trashy book about Hackwill which became a hit movie. Now the monster was persecuting him.

There was a scene where Adam argued with his girlfriend – Hedley! – and she walked out.

'Adam,' Hedley spat, 'this is nothing to do with you, but there's nothing for me here.'

Everything was twisted around. Really, Lesley left amicably, sadly confessing that she couldn't keep up. Her main reason for going was that her Mum was sick. They weren't definitely finished.

'It's not about money either,' Hedley snarled, throwing a bottle. 'It's a quality of life decision.'

In the film, Adam slapped Hedley around and tossed her out of the house, yelling abuse. The movie woman wasn't like Lesley; she was an older tramp who kept Adam in cocaine and got drunk in the daytime. Adam Kiss, a thoroughgoing bastard, wasn't like Allan Keyes.

A sad, complicated situation was turned into trite soap.

Hackwill made Hedley shrink while on a binge so she literally drowned in a gin bottle. After that, Adam got mixed up with Shelley, a Hollywood madame Allan recognised as the Devil Princess, and embarked on a crusade of degeneracy that allowed for edge-of-hardcore sex scenes interspersed with blubbering hysterical breakdowns. Hackwill stalked the feckless, worthless, useless Adam Kiss. Supporting characters died.

Allan looked from the screen to the Screamin' Rob and back again. He couldn't understand how New Frontier had allowed this to happen. His lawyers would take the company to pieces.

You didn't do anything. You're innocent. You're not Adam Kiss.

Covering all the sleaze bases, *Hackwill's Back!* stirred in elements from the Roman Polanski and Rob Lowe sex scandals. Adam was videotaped in an orgy with two extremely underaged girls. Allan found the scene deeply disturbing. As Ellen Jeanette's camera got excited and the Heavy Metal throbbed like a painful erection, the image went in and out of focus and Allan kept seeing his own features instead of the actor's. The speakers behind the screen shrieked.

Hackwill was looming. The monster stepped in, steel claws flashing, and he gutted the girls, covering the screaming Adam-Allan with insides.

After the blood settled, a phone rang in the murder room, and Hackwill reached for it to make a joke.

The real phone rang, shocking Allan into action. He grabbed out for it, stabbing the pause button. Adam's face froze, dripping.

'*Enjoying the show?*' Hackwill croaked.

'Mal, you bastard, is this you? You didn't tell me about *Hackwill's Back!* I'll take Calme for everything.'

'*Silly Daddy, this isn't Mal-de-merde. This is Rob.*'

Allan froze, feeling the warm wetness on his own face. Numbed, he slipped into his own darkness.

He woke up in a wash of pain. Bloody pulses shot through his brain. His sinuses were sandpapery and his gums hurt. He tasted rinds of whisky blood between his teeth.

Allan had got half-way out of the video room and was twisted in a static-crackly sheet. He was out of his clothes and sticky all over. He'd just lie here for a moment and hope he wasn't about to be sick.

The projection video buzzed.

He sat up, getting the door-jamb behind his back, and the sheet fell away from his chest. There was bruising around his right nipple. He touched the spot and it hurt. It was as if a powerful vacuum cleaner had been stuck to his tit.

His back was scratched and trickling. He thought he felt splinters of raw wood in there. Trying to remember, his head fogged.

Heavy night, Adam?

'That's not me,' he said, his voice ancient, 'that's the other fellow.'

He still wore his $15,000 watch. It was 08:22. At nine, Amaranth would be here. And Consuela, who cleaned. Looking into the video room, he saw Consuela would earn a bonus today. The place was almost wrecked. Furniture overturned, empty bottles broken and trodden into the rugs, clothes scattered. Even pictures hung crooked. The blinding white of the screen upon which light was still projecting was splashed with something that dried to brown-orange.

He remembered *Hackwill's Back!* and he remembered being angry. He must have cut loose.

I guess this is that Lifestyle of the Rich and Famous you always wanted.

Unwinding himself from the sheet, he found he was wearing a condom.

As he slipped it off, it squelched.

Somebody had a good time last night.

It was as if he'd skipped a couple of days. He had come home, watched half a video, got angry, fallen asleep. Checking his watch again, he confirmed that it was the next morning.

He couldn't even remember a debauched dream. In his night thoughts, he'd been at school again naked, sitting an exam he hadn't prepared for, chased by bullies, trying to wrap a parcel that came apart in his hands. A wet dream would have been a relief.

In the bathroom, he dealt with the condom. Two others floated in the toilet. Like a persistent turd, one took three flushes to vanish.

Looking in the mirror, he was alarmed by red streaks around his mouth. Tasting, he realised it was lipstick. He washed the stuff off, easing grit out of his eyes, and extensively brushed his teeth. He wanted a shower but it was 08:33; he should check the rest of the house before Amaranth and Consuela arrived. He didn't want any more surprises.

He pulled on a bathrobe (a ratty Marks & Spencer garment that had come all the way from Somerset to Beverly Hills) and stalked back to the video room. Some of the clothes on the floor, and distributed around the furniture, were obviously not his.

A pair of diaphanous panties hung over the Screamin' Hackwill. Allan saw his monster's snarl through the thin material. He whipped them away. A cursory search found a single white ankle sock, a violently pink halter top and a studded leather item that was either a belt for a very thin person or a wristlet for a very fat one. In an ashtray, speckled with grey fluff, was a half-sucked lollipop. Also three cardboard-and-rizla-and-spit lumps he recognised from his film school days as roaches.

Outwardly, Allan Keyes is a normal, well-adjusted individual, not at all like the monsters he creates. But after dark, he turns into a raging party beast, a pervert who loves to be whipped with a pony-tail, a sad swinger with a taste for illegally young flesh...

08:47.

He would think about this later. Now, he needed a bin-liner for all the ...

evidence?

... for all the alien articles. Something strange was happening, and he needed to re-establish control.

As he worked through the house (whatever happened had been confined to the downstairs rooms, it seemed) Allan became more aware of the memories of his body. He discovered interesting new aches and pains. He might have thrown his neck out.

08:56.

Done.

You have been.

One last look at the video room. Divan upright, cushions in order, stuff wiped off screen, pictures straightened, floor picked clear. Any suspicious stains were nothing more than Ovaltine.

09:01.

He didn't insist on exact time-keeping. But he heard the beeping of the security override and a bustle out in the hall that he associated with Consuela. She listened constantly to salsa on a walkman and unconsciously hummed along with it.

The video remote control lay on the divan. He picked it up and stabbed at EJECT but missed and hit PLAY.

It was the orgy scene from *Hackwill's Back!* Adam Kiss and the two underage girls. Body-parts pumped in close-up. He was sure the breasts came from a different film.

Consuela shrilled a 'good morning' from the next room.

The New Frontier quality was appalling. He could swear this was video, not film. The image was fixed, as if someone had dropped a camcorder and let the tape play on. From a skewed perspective, Adam Kiss entered a squealing girl from behind.

Is this supposed to be sexy? The MPAA will never let this through. She looks about twelve.

The image moved again, as if the other girl had picked up the camera, and then zoomed shakily towards Adam.

This isn't film, this is video.

And it wasn't Adam.

Knowing at last that something was definitely broken inside his head, Allan was unable to freeze the image. He was fascinated by his own distorted face. It *was* him but he wasn't like that.

He wasn't.

The screen Allan lost his stroke and grinned at the camera, then, biting his lips, started to thrust again. A girl said 'you're hurting me' and Allan said 'good'.

Consuela walked in.

'I no longer consider myself purely a horror writer,' Allan told Mockridge, 'I'm not sure I was ever really comfortable in the category. I mean, if you compare what I do to Steve King or Dean Koontz, you'll see...'

'That doesn't sound like the Man Who Made Rob Hackwill.'

'Turner, let's put it like this: the genre can be comfortable. Too comfortable. It's at once a cradle and a trap.'

'It's been a while since *Cornworld*. What will your next book project be? Will it be horror?'

'It's kind of a magical fantasia with a Gulf War subtext. I'm not quite sure of the direction it'll take at the moment.'

'What about *Hackwill's Back!*? What did *you* think?'

Allan's fixed grin must have been distinctly Hackwillian.

'Well, Ray Calme and I are *talking* again. We had a rough patch, but he's the first one to admit that the sequel strayed from the path somewhat?'

'Will there be a *Part III*?'

'*Hackwill's Back!*, without getting a single positive review, grossed $20,000,000 *more* than *Where the Bodies Are Buried* theatrically. The kids who saw the first one only on tape or cable bought tickets to the follow-up. With figures like that, there will certainly be a *Part III*. Nothing I can do will stop it.'

'And will you be involved?'

'There are business questions still unanswered. I doubt very much, with *Cornworld* on the go again, that I could schedule a gig, even if New Frontier offered it to me. But Ray always wants me to be involved.'

'And the *Hackwill's Horrors* TV show?'

'If there is one, it's news to me.'

Somehow, Allan kept a lid on things. He *still* didn't know what had happened that night (and, as it was, didn't want to know) but, though he had trouble hiring another domestic, he'd not gone down in a blaze of supermarket tabloids and morals clauses. Fleeing-the-country-at-midnight careericide had not taken place.

He had burned the cassette. Still labelled *Hackwill's Back!*, it'd been recorded over. Occasionally, he wondered if he shouldn't have kept it for further examination. It must have been faked. He knew technology existed to lay in his face on someone else's sex scene.

And your moles? Your appendix scar?

He tentatively investigated the possibility of a libel suit, taking a lawyer associated with his new agency to an advance screening of *Where the Bodies Are Buried, Part II*. The smart young woman politely thought he was crazy, and Allan had to agree with her.

The film they saw was nothing like the one on the tape, the one that had been wiped over. It was the high school story he'd read in the script, about Hackwill possessing a geeky teenager. It was also not very good. The for-one-night-only, special-for-Allan Keyes *Hackwill's Back!* had been a better piece of film-making.

He did not return calls from Ellen Jeanette Sheridan.

The Hackwill Juggernaut rolled on. Martin H. Greenberg edited a shared-world paperback anthology in which leading horror writers from Karl Edward Wagner to Philip Nutman explored the 'Rob Hackwill Mythos'; Allan allowed the reprint of 'A Trickle of Shame' but refused to rewrite it to make it consistent with the film version. New Frontier *was* producing *Hackwill's Horrors*, a cable TV anthology hosted by Mal Gariazzo in monster make-up. Though TV rights had been signed away in the initial contract, New Frontier allotted fully two-thirds of the script budget for the show to buying the rights to a couple of stories from *Strange Segments*.

As weeks and months passed, he no longer expected a sudden eruption of furious parents, sobbing girls and vice cops. A hurricane had passed and would never return. *Cornworld* was put back and back.

'No more writer-directors,' Calme promised. 'Well, no more writer-directors who aren't Allan Keyes.'

Allan shrugged, non-committal. He was doing lunch as a favour to Mal Gariazzo. Like a child of divorce forever trying to manipulate his parents into a reconciliation, Gariazzo was constantly nagging Allan and Calme to get back together.

'The next Bodies has got to be a wow or the franchise is a bust,' Gariazzo insisted.

'I hear Ellen Jeanette has a three-picture deal,' Allan said.

'Positive discrimination will get you a long way in this town,' Calme suggested, waving away the memory of *Hackwill's Back!*

Their waiter brought drinks out to the terrace. Clogged with greenery, the restaurant annex was like a standing set from a Tarzan movie. To blend in, Calme wore a Banana Republic shirt of the type popular among moguls with paunches. Everyone in the room wore shades of pastel.

'When does *Cornworld* start?' Gariazzo asked.

Allan mumbled a harrumph but Calme saved his explanation by laying out his cards.

'Just give us a concept, Allan,' he said. 'We'll have it developed into a story, then machined into a script. You'll have approval at every stage. We have a line on a 3-D process that doesn't give you a headache. And we've got this incredible Icelander to direct.'

'*Icelander?*'

'Snordlij Svensson,' Gariazzo put in. 'He made an action movie, *American Atrocity*, out of nothing.'

Allan shrugged.

'We want you back, Allan,' Calme said. 'The fans want you. Breeze says she'll only do the Devil Princess for you. The East Coast needs your name.'

'*Rob Hackwill* wants you,' Gariazzo said, finally.

It was an insane situation. On the one hand, Allan was two rewrites away from a green light on *Cornworld*, a $45,000,000 and up Summer picture he thought guaranteed Huge. On the other, he could pick up $100,000 pocket change by grinding out three pages of notes for a *Part III in 3-D* that was almost certain to be an embarrassment.

There was no reason he couldn't do both. But somehow, he wasn't doing either.

The new novel, *The Great Satan*, had come out of a bidding war with a million *pound* advance from Real Press; but he was only three chapters in, and finding it heavier going than before. Reluctantly, he was on the point of conceding that he couldn't possibly meet his deadline and would have to make a research trip to Bagdhad as soon as the ruins stopped smoking. He couldn't believe that, six years ago, he'd written the 14,000 words of 'A Trickle of Shame' in a single day. On a manual typewriter.

The more you pull, the tighter the knot gets.

Finally, one night, late, he wrote a concept for *Part III in 3-D*. It had been there all the time, waiting. As he word-processed, he found himself chortling Gariazzo's Hackwill laugh. His concept, if he could call it 'his', was about Adam Kiss, a tabloid reporter who'd covered up the original murder of Rob Hackwill, then churned out a supermarket paperback about the dead blackmailer's crimes. Having developed a taste for perverse high life, Adam was open to exposure when Hackwill returned yet again from Hell to rip his life apart. Everyone around Adam died in gruesome ways; Allan didn't even bother to specify them, knowing New Frontier's effects bods probably had dozens of extra freak deaths they'd never been able to work into a film and would love to shove in here. Finally, Adam took the blame for the whole thing and was dragged off, protesting his worthless innocence, to death row where, in a last-scene kicker, the man who pulled the switch was Hackwill himself. There were no sympathetic characters, but that was a problem for whoever turned the concept into a story.

He felt entitled to the Adam Kiss Story; it was *his* psychotic episode, he had the right to turn it into money.

With it out of his system, the words started flowing again. He turned around a *Cornworld* rewrite and had it in with Pyramid, then had a major breakthrough on *The Great Satan*. Once he stopped thinking of it, even subconsciously, as a horror novel, the whole thing took shape and developed its own forward momentum. Occasionally, he would try out new-coined category descriptions, seeing how comfortable he was with them: *Nouveau* Gothic, Mainstream *Guignol*, Slaughterpunk, Metaphysical Realism. This time, he was really reaching. Sometimes, he felt as if he were back in the coffee-and-pills rush of *Chitinous Splinters* or the *Strange Segments* stories, back before the career millstones had been tied around his neck. In idle moments, he pondered his Booker Prize acceptance speech. And his graceful thanks to the Academy of Motion Picture Arts and Sciences.

The day he got a start date for *Cornworld*, he insisted his credit on *Where the Bodies Are Buried, Part III in 3-D* be changed from 'original screen story by Allan Keyes' to 'based on concepts created by Allan Keyes'. Like a President, he wanted 'plausible deniability' if the Wizard of Rekjavik turned out a howling dog like *Hackwill's Back!* New Frontier went along with it.

In a letter to Lesley, he said that, for a while, he felt he had lost the reins of his career; now, he was back in charge. 'I write the stories,' he said, 'they don't write me.'

*

'I don't see why I should have to justify myself, Turner. *The Great Satan* is not a horror novel. I've never written horror, I've always written *Allan Keyes*. There has been some overlap. This time, I want to go a different way. It's not like I've betrayed a religion. I just want to say something. There are people I can't reach with horror and I need them for this one. There is some major league ass that I have a burning compulsion to kick. Trust me, I've never broken my covenant with the fans yet.'

'And *Cornworld*?'

'What can I say? We lost the corn. We had fields lined up in Canada but Costner couldn't commit this summer and the harvest came along. I guess we'll be back again next year.'

'And you'll still direct?'

'There is no question of me not directing *Cornworld*, Turner. It's my baby.'

A sly light burned in Mockridge's pale eyes. He came to the next question.

'What *Fango* is really interested in, of course, is *Bodies III*. Will it really be in 3-D?'

'You'll have to ask New Frontier about that. I've not been in communication with them for a while. Whatever happens, it can't be worse than *Hackwill's Back!*'

'What do you mean, "insurance problems"?'

Allan had Everson Deeming, his new agent, on the speaker-phone. As he listened, his hands made fists.

'Allan, I've been delving. My informant at Pyramid tells me there's been a change in the climate. Since the buy-out, it's been musical chairs in the executive suite.'

Derek Leech, the multi-media magnate, had just bought Pyramid. He already owned Real Press, so he was a majority shareholder in Allan Keyes.

'But *Cornworld* is still go?'

'Indubitably. But, in strictest confidence, they've been talking with Ellen Jeanette Sheridan.'

Ellen Jeanette had waltzed off the *Hackwill's Back!* fiasco into *Laughing Boy*, a medium-budget action romance about a housewife and a private eye. The film made a new male star, re-established a fading female one and passed the $100,000,000 mark in domestic gross.

'I'm pay-or-play, right?'

'Yes but they can pay you *not* to direct.'

'If they do, someone dies.'

'That's not a very helpful remark.'

The buzz was that Ellen Jeanette was close to signing with Allan's new agency.

You should have been good to me, Allan. People who are good to me get on in life...

The Great Satan was nearly finished. It *was* good, it *was* important. Real Press swallowed their objections and were gearing for a promotion massive enough to recoup their investment. Everybody knew there would be controversy; feelings about the War still ran high everywhere, and Allan Keyes had been no respecter of feelings.

He would not give up *Cornworld* without a fight. Loretta Grange, his new new agent, said she could fight his contract up to the Supreme Court. If he didn't direct, it didn't happen.

And Rob Hackwill was *everywhere*. He had daily interview requests; always to talk about Hackwill, never the rest of his work. Critical articles claimed Hackwill represented the Dark Underside of the American Dream. Televangelists, who hadn't forgiven him for Julian Sands, preached that Hackwill lead American teenagers into Satanism. New Frontier went into licensing frenzy: there were Hackwill action figures, make-up kits, pop-up books, video games, jokes, T-shirts, posters, lunch-boxes, parade floats, novelty records, soundtrack CDs, stationery, soft toys, condoms.

Sometimes it seemed as if Rob Hackwill had made Allan Keyes.

But, without you, Allan, I'm not me*! These merchants don't understand the real Rob Hackwill. You didn't mean me to be cuddly, you didn't mean me to be a comedian. When will I be a* monster *again?*

He picked up the phone and heard the familiar chortle, echoing straight from Hell.

'Who is this?' he fairly shrieked. 'Why can't you leave me... '

'Relax, relax,' said Mal Gariazzo. 'It's just an actor.'

Allan made up an excuse about crank calls. Gariazzo had been to enough *Fangoria* conventions to understand. Some people were seriously sick out there.

'You free tonight?' Gariazzo asked.

'What's up?'

'The first answer print of *Where the Bodies Are Buried, Part III in 3-D*. I'm screening it at the house. Even Ray Calme hasn't seen it yet. And I've got an extra pair of 3-D glasses with your name on them.'

'I really don't know...'

Gariazzo did the voice again. *'What's the matter? Scared, are we?'*

The actor was identifying too closely with the part, Allan thought. *He'll have to be reminded who the real Rob Hackwill is.*

'I think you'll be surprised,' Gariazzo said. 'Snordlij Svensson is a genius.'

'I'll be over.'

Gariazzo's mansion wasn't finished. Half the house was covered with plastic sheets, concealing exposed wooden bones that had yet to be fleshed with plaster. The backyard was an excavation site which would be turned into a pool.

Rob Hackwill had made Mal Gariazzo prosperous. When he signed for *Where the Bodies Are Buried*, he'd been living in a rooming house in Ventura and doing shopping channel voice-overs.

In the foyer, currently paved with yellow newspapers, a bigger-than-life Hackwill stood to greet visitors. Gariazzo posed beside it when Allan entered, as if ready for a publicity still.

Gariazzo was hyper, a couple of snorts into happyland. He showed Allan through the place, describing what would be where and how much it would cost. In one room, Gariazzo had more Hackwill merchandise than a Halloween sale. He had the phonecards from Japan, the Christmas tree ornaments, the velvet portraits, the stained glass windows, the cookie mixes.

I'm spread too thin, Daddy. I'm leaking away in cheap tat.

The basement 'romper room' was outfitted with a large bed and lots of strange devices Allan imagined were sexual implements. Gariazzo, with his choice of gothic groupies, no longer had a problem getting laid, and his priapic activities at conventions were becoming industry gossip. Allan heard Gariazzo had serviced Ellen Jeanette in order to get more close-ups on *Hackwill's Back!*

The screening room was finished. Gariazzo ran the projector himself. Allan settled, adjusting the 3-D glasses as the New Frontier logo thrust out from the screen. Hellish violet murk swirled and green letters formed.

'"All spirits are enslaved that serve things evil" – Shelley.'

Shelley! A bit high-fa-fuckin-lutin' for New Frontier!

The familiar *Where the Bodies Are Buried* title emerged from the murk, and then *Part III in 3-D* shot out like a clawed hand. Allan cringed in his seat. He heard Gariazzo chortling. There was no longer a difference between the actor's laugh and the monster's.

In the first scene, the camera crept through a cemetery to discover a dark figure violating an unmarked grave. This was where the town fathers had buried Hackwill after they tortured and killed him, and the site of the exorcism finale of *Hackwill's Back!* Gravestones loomed in 3-D, sheets of rain cut down. Svensson was certainly a good picture-maker. This had a richness, a quality far in excess of the first sequel. Objectively, *Part III in 3-D* looked better than *Where the Bodies Are Buried.*

The earth was removed from the grave and the rotted but still whole body of Hackwill was disclosed to the night. In a flash of lightning, the monster's distorted face flared with evil dead life. The make-up had been redesigned, to stand closer scrutiny. It was wetter, more complicated, more expressive than the simple mask Allan had worked around on the original.

'That's me,' Gariazzo giggled. 'I insisted on being buried, not the stuntman.'

The grave-robber picked Hackwill up by the shoulders and flipped him over, ramming his face into the wet earth. Lighting struck again, the effect paling from overuse. The grave-robber produced a bayonet, slowly drawing it from a scabbard. This being 3-D, the weapon thrust obscenely at the camera, its point seeming to hover nine yards out of the screen. Allan's eyeballs tried to revolve.

Gariazzo whooed as if on a rollercoaster.

This clown is beginning to irritate me.

The grave-robber, face still in darkness, stripped Hackwill's corpse of dirt as if he were undressing a lover. Then he stabbed deep into the dead body, opening up a hole in the small of the monster's back. The gash seeped blood.

Then a reverse shot showed the violator's face. It was Allan. Not an actor playing Adam Kiss, but Allan himself. He looked at his own face in 3-D and wondered how – and why? – the trick had been done.

The 3-D Allan unbuttoned his long coat and slipped it off. He was naked to the waist, with stereoscopic gooseflesh. Allan recognised his own scars, the patterns of his body hair. Again, the world was dizzyingly out of joint.

Allan pulled off his 3-D glasses and gripped his face. An ache had set in behind the bridge of his nose. The polarised image was fuzzy and rainbowed. He looked at the screen and saw something different. A clothed actor he recognised. Brion James, the great B picture villain. Even the scene was different.

He put the glasses back on and saw himself in the graveyard. His head buzzed, but he had to watch. The 3-D Allan made a fist and thrust it out of the screen. Allan cringed at the effect.

The film which seemed to be projected only in his head continued. Allan Keyes fell upon Hackwill and mightily thrust his fist into the aperture, burrowing up through the corpse's spine. The images were explicit, and disgusting. The film Allan reached in beyond his elbow, making a ghastly glove puppet of the monster. In close-ups, steel-clawed hands became rigid and razored. Allan was sure he would see himself gutted by his creation, but the monster eased himself gently out of the earth and was helped out of the grave. Hackwill's single red eye glowed with malign intelligence, Allan's hand lodged somewhere inside his head.

Allan lifted his glasses again. The real film was continuing, with Gariazzo-as-Hackwill stalking James-as-Kiss. It was stylish and it had a plot. Gariazzo had drifted into a happy baby daze.

The 3-D mind movie continued. The film Allan and the real Hackwill, under whose rotten face Mal Gariazzo did not lurk, left the graveyard and walked into town. It wasn't the Anywhere, USA, of *Where the Bodies Are Buried*, but the real West Country town where Allan had grown up, where he had set 'A Trickle of Shame'.

Creator and monster, joined by flesh and blood, made their way through familiar streets. There was the Corn Exchange, the Palace, Denbeigh Gardens, Brink's Cafe. A poster for the council elections cried 'VOTE HACKWILL'. Finally, the camera climbed familiar stairs up above a shop to a familiar flat. The film Allan had lost his keys, so he rapped on the door. After fumbling, Lesley answered and let him in. Her eyes literally bulged in surprise as the bayonet rammed into her stomach and she was lifted off her feet...

*

When consciousness returned, Allan found himself naked on bare bedsprings, smeared with something sticky and smelly. One arm was wrenched back behind his head, shoulder joint straining, and his wrist was circled. Craning, he saw upside-down, that he was handcuffed to a knotched black wooden post above the bed. The image was fuzzily strange. He was still wearing his 3-D glasses. Concealed lighting flashed on and off, filling the room with lavalamp swirls.

Something heavy weighed on his midriff. His nose stung and his mouth was thick with a terrible taste.

Somewhere, Hackwill was laughing.

'Get off,' he said, bucking his hips to dislodge the person draped across him.

The body came free and, in strobing light, Allan saw Mal Gariazzo's staring face through plastic. A bag was fixed over his head and twist-tied at his neck. The actor wore only a black string vest. His torso was smeared with blood.

Allan shifted himself and found the handcuff loose enough to slip out of. He got off the bed. The imprint of the springs must be on his back and bottom. He was covered in someone else's blood.

A bore-hole had been made in Mal Gariazzo's back, and used. It was quite shallow and had not displaced anything vital. It was the hood that had killed the actor.

There can be only one.

There were older marks on Gariazzo's body, where he had been cut before. Real scars looked nothing like the latex on Hackwill's face.

'I didn't do anything,' Allan said, aloud.

M'lud, while I concede that my client was found with the victim's blood generously plastered over his body and that Mr Gariazzo's wallet was in Mr Keyes's back pocket at the time of arrest, I'm sure his previous good character will be taken into account.

'Shut yer neck,' Allan shouted.

It was 05:09. Allan looked at the mess. There was no question of cleaning any fingerprints he might have left. The room, probably the house, was liberally smeared with his dabs.

If you're serious about concealing evidence, your best bet would be to torch the place. Sure, in this weather, the fire might spread and other people might die, but they can't gas you twice...

Allan had never had his fingerprints taken. They weren't on file anywhere. He'd been alone in the house with Gariazzo. Nobody had seen him arrive. No one would see him leave. Nothing could put him at the scene.

'And, what's more, I'm innocent.'

He found his clothes neatly piled on a rack by the door, folded exactly as his mother taught him. He dressed, uncomfortably aware of filth between skin and underwear, and shoved his cardboard glasses into a pocket. He darted from the house to his car, which had been in the garage out of sight, and drove unobtrusively out of the neighbourhood. This being California, there were no pedestrians to remember him. Early morning light made everything look polarised.

Home and dry, killer?

Only as he neared his own house, red flakes of dried blood falling from his face and scalp like gory dandruff, did his insides relax. His worrying brain patterns kicked in again.

Someone was dead, someone was responsible. *And it wasn't Allan Keyes!*

He got back to his mansion and stripped for a shower. Warm jets washed him as clean as his conscience.

After *Hackwill's Back!*, no schoolgirls had come forward and testified to being in an orgy with him. After *Part III in 3-D*, no corpse would make him out to be a murderer.

If this was the same as the last time, the physical evidence would be misleading. Gariazzo probably wasn't dead. Allan had just lived through his own imaginary *Part III in 3-D*. In the real world, *Where the Bodies Are Buried, Part III in 3-D* was a story about Adam Kiss as played by Brion James. Mal Gariazzo would be happily taping his pun-filled links for *Hackwill's Horrors* and looking through his black book of starlet wannabes in search of a target for tonight.

The phone rang just as Allan got out of the shower.

Bad news.

It was too early. Even if it had happened, Gariazzo wouldn't have been found yet. It must be something else.

So few people have this number, though.

'Cut it out, or in the next sequel – which I'll personally write – I'll reincarnate you as a fluffy pink bunny rabbit and have you befriended by Macaulay Culkin.'

He got to the phone before the machine cut in. It was his mother, with terrible, terrible news. About Lesley.

'I'm sorry, babe,' Loretta said, voice tinny from New York, 'but publishing is a conservative business. The chairman himself, Derek Leech, has ruled on *The Great Satan*. Real Press will not publish, and I quote, "a love letter to Saddam Hussein".'

'But that's ridiculous. Leech can't have read the book properly. The hero is a *dissident* Iraqi, for heaven's sake.'

'We're not talking rational, babe, we're talking rich.'

It seemed horribly possible Allan would have to return a million pounds. His contract was ambiguous on the point.

'There are other publishers and there's lots of interest. You're enough of a name to ensure that. In the long run, this will help. Controversy sells books.'

Allan swallowed rage.

'It looks like Leech will become hands-on in Pyramid,' Loretta continued. 'With the *Cornworld* situation so delicate, it probably wasn't a good time for him to sour on Allan Keyes.'

'I didn't do this on purpose. I just wrote an honest book.'

Like Salman Rushdie, eh?

'Contrary to what they told you in school, babe, honesty sometimes is not the best policy.'

The phlegmatic Los Angeles coroner ruled Mal Gariazzo's death as 'accidental, due to sexual experiment'. New Frontier launched a search for 'the new Rob Hackwill'. The West Somerset Constabulary were following several promising leads, but no suspects at this time were sought for questioning with regard to the murder of Lesley Conyers. One of the tackier supermarket papers asked him if he felt the violence in his books and films contributed to the moral climate which created monsters like the fiend who had killed his girlfriend. Allan had scared the reptile off with a Hackwill look.

Where the *Bodies Are Buried, Part III in 3-D* outgrossed both earlier *Bodies* films put together and Snordlij Svensson was attached to several major projects. Sean Connery and Kevin Costner were keen to work with him. Sales of Mal Gariazzo Memorial Hackwill merchandise were heavier than could have been predicted.

Allan sat at home and didn't answer the telephone.

He watched *Chitinous Splinters* on video, over and over, and saw other paths he might have taken, leading into the world of art cinema rather than the bloodied fields of genre. He reread *Strange Segments* over and over. Not just 'A Trickle of Shame', but all the other stories. Some of the prose was rough but he was surprised by their strength. He could see the seeds of *The Great Satan*, his unpublished (unpublishable?) masterpiece, already germinating. He regretted his overuse of the Cosmic Justice formula, though.

Now, as each day drew a noose tighter, he felt he was *living* through an EC horror comic plot, and that he was the protagonist. But there was a difference, a cosmic injustice which he needed to appeal to the highest court.

He hadn't done anything wrong.

'I'd like to talk about rumours that you're working on a fourth *Bodies* script? The title that has been leaked is *The Redevelopment: Where the Bodies Are Buried 4*.'

'I'm sorry, Mockridge. I can't schedule an interview now.'

'But –'

'Just fuck off and get a life you little anorak.'

The dead line buzzed in his hand. He had sounded more than ever like Hackwill.

He was acting as his own agent. He could hardly do a worse job than the dead-weights he'd been stuck with.

'If it were me, *I'd* have you direct, but you understand the East Coast Boys...'

Calme let that hang.

The new script was on the desk. *The Redevelopment*. Allan might have to work with New Frontier's in-house rewrite man. He was getting a flat $15,000. That was more than he had earned for his first two books, five years of solid work, but now it felt like an insult.

'It's terrible about Mal, but fans don't care who's under the mask. Hackwill is the star of the *Bodies* franchise. And Hackwill can't die.'

Allan sat quietly. Writing *The Redevelopment* was like taking dictation. He listened to the voice and wrote it down.

'No jokes in this one,' Calme said. 'It'll be serious, scary. Like *Bodies One*. No French teacher in the hot tub. We've got away from your original concept and I'm glad you're back. Rob Hackwill without Allan Keyes is not the same monster. Things have been rough, but we will endure.'

The Redevelopment would be dedicated to Gariazzo. The fans would expect no less.

At first, Allan had not been interested in working on the sequel. He had other irons in the fire. He could get meetings at any of the Majors. But Calme told him he had talked with Gariazzo the night before he died and that the actor had told him he was expecting company. There was no question of anyone accusing Allan of anything. But it would be tidier if Calme kept secrets.

It'll be you and me, Allan. Forever.

Calme paged through the script. He came to the last scene. After the climax, in the graveyard, something stirred. A hook. The producer smiled, sequels yet unborn stirring in his eyes, and congratulated Allan on anticipating his needs.

Allan could feel the hook, in his own flesh. It was a tiny pinprick, among many tiny pinpricks. The hooks were endless. There would be further sequels. Next would be *Hackwill's End: The Last Body*, followed by *Where the Bodies Are Buried 6: The Next Degeneration*, *Where the Bodies Are Buried VII: Devil Bride of Rob Hackwill...*

And Allan Keyes was yoked to the wheel that would grind on and on. He knew now he was enslaved and that his punishment was just. He had brought evil into the world and betrayed it. That evil was now his master. Hackwill was his responsibility, and everything else he had written, everything else he had filmed, everything else he had done, was a cosmic irrelevance.

Think of it, Allan, Hackwill X, Part XXXVI, Part MCMLIV ... *Spiral stories without beginning, without end, a ritual of retribution re-enacted as long as there are graves and corpses and secrets and sins...*

'If we play this right, Allan, it can run and run and run...'

WHERE THE BODIES ARE BURIED 3:
BLACK AND WHITE AND RED ALL OVER

He thought his wide suit made him look like a useless boyfriend in a '70s sit-com. Not Scobie's idea of a good time but Harry insisted his reporters be smart. 'We're a local paper,' Harry always said, 'we have to be acceptable to local people.' The editor also insisted his reporters' hair be neither too short nor too long. Working for the *Herald* was like doing National Service.

At his desk, playing cat's cradle with elastic bands, Iain Scobie dreamed of Fleet Street. Rather, he dreamed of London Docklands. Most nationals had quit the Street. Papers like the *Comet* and the *Argus* were published from the Docklands Pyramid of Leech International.

He was resigned to serving out years in this West Country backwater before he was summoned by Derek Leech to join the thrusting dynamo of the *Comet*. Unless a horse came along: a story he could ride all the way to the finish line.

The *Herald*'s one eccentricity, which no one dared joke about to its editor's face, was Harry's enthusiasm for stories about the Girl Guides. An edition never passed without a picture of some pigtailed pixie covered in mud for charity creeping into the first three pages.

Scobie had recently manoeuvred a promotion from fêtes and school pantos to crime. In this town, crime meant broken pub windows, missing bicycle lamps and scrumped apples. When a New Age convoy crept near, he'd thought it might be his horse, but the police diverted the travellers into swamped moorland with no fuss at all.

'Time for a cup of rosie lee,' Harry announced, having finished his editorial about council car parks. He looked about for someone who could be forced into tea-making. Scobie let go and bands twanged into space, stinging his fingers.

'Iain,' Harry said, pronouncing the second 'i' which often got left out of Scobie's by-line, 'could you bestir yourself kettle-wards.'

Scobie's telephone rang.

'Important call, Harry,' Scobie said, picking up. Actually, the call was unlikely to be anything. Another cow wedged in a ditch. A bid to twin the town with a pile of war-torn rubble in the former Soviet Union. A cancelled Carnival concert.

It was Greg Dunphy, a police constable Scobie bought pints for. Both liked to pretend Scobie was a journalist and Dunphy a valuable source.

'I've got summat,' Dunphy said.

From the lack of preliminary when-is-the-next-skittles-match-and-piss-up? farting-around, he could tell Dunphy really had something he was forced to take seriously. Scobie heard the faint neighing of a wild horse, ready to be roped and broken and rough-ridden to the *Comet*.

On the Achelzoy road, about two miles beyond of the town limits, Scobie found the car, an anonymous white Honda. It looked to have been badly parked rather than crashed. Its front stuck over the roadside ditch, wheels in mud. Dunphy's bike leant against the phone box. The policeman stood by the car. The girl sat on the grass, as if for a picnic. Dunphy must have radioed the station before he called Scobie – it took a lot more rounds to earn the kind of loyalty that made coppers call a reporter before his sergeant – but Scobie had arrived first.

He parked the Skoda – the *Herald*'s car, not his choice – and got out. Dunphy, almost hopping, was relieved to see him. The constable was completely out of his depth, terrified of messing up.

'Iain, watch this girl.'

She was under twenty and wore a white dress. Blonde hair pinned back. Pretty without being sexy. Wholesome. Harry would love to run a picture of her in a Girl Guide uniform.

Dunphy hopped towards a bush. The policeman had been bursting for a pee. Scobie looked at the girl, who smiled openly, then at the car.

'I wasn't careless,' she said. 'Swerved to miss a rabbit.'

A police car, siren shrilling, drew up next to Scobie's Skoda. Sergeant Sloman had his driver cut off the racket and walked over, not pleased to see Scobie. Dunphy came back, relieved, but was shaken at his sergeant's arrival when he was off the scene.

'You,' Sloman said, pointing. 'Go home.'

Scobie got out his press card.

'That doesn't say "Get Out of Jail Free" scumshine.'

He backed off but did not make a move towards the Skoda. Sloman stood by the girl and thought things over.

Scobie recognised her. School nurse at Ash Grove Comprehensive. He'd interviewed her about a rumoured epidemic of headlice. It had come to nothing. Her name was Elizabeth Yatman.

'Where are the others, Elizabeth?' asked Sloman.

She said nothing.

Sloman's driver poked around Elizabeth's car. He opened the passenger door and a bundle fell out. A white face stuck out of blanket swaddling. The bundle looked like a big baby.

Sloman's driver was sick.

'Where are the others, Elizabeth?'

The Honda was ringed with police cars, as if an armed terrorist were at the wheel. The road was coned across in both directions. Diversion signs were up. Sloman had the cordon established so quickly Scobie was trapped *inside* rather than kept out. Not wanting to admit a mistake, Sloman (also out of his depth) let him stick around providing he didn't get in the way.

There was confusion about what to do. Sloman felt Elizabeth's car and the horrid bundle shouldn't be moved until a lot more policemen had looked them over, but that still left him with Elizabeth herself. She was smiling and co-operative unless asked a direct question. Anyone coming on the scene would assume she was a victim or a witness...

That would be a good first line. 'Anyone coming on the scene would assume Elizabeth Yatman was a victim or a witness, not the alleged murderer of one child and a suspect in the disappearance of eight others...' Not 'assume'. That wasn't a newspaper word.

As afternoon faded, gloom gathered. It was quite warm for Autumn, but a chill was coming. Policemen milled about, directionless. The Backwater Plods were waiting for the Pros from Dover.

Scobie slid into the Skoda and locked the doors. He bent low and dug out his cellular phone. He could dictate to the *Herald*'s copy-taker. Even Harry would tear the car park decision off the front page to make room for Elizabeth Yatman.

He stabbed Autodial #1, then cut off half-way through the clicks. This was his horse. He shouldn't lead it to the wrong stable. Loading his phone's memory with numbers, he'd been able to think of only nine he used regularly. The extra space, he hopefully filled with a number he would like to use regularly. He stabbed Autodial #0.

The phone was instantly answered.

'*Daily Comet*, how may I help you?'

At first, the *Comet* wanted to send down their own stringer from Bristol, but Scobie bargained hard. He was on the spot and had a head start. Unless he got to file his own copy, he'd go to the next tabloid on the list. The phone-answerer transferred him up through several desks to Ronald Clewes, the *Comet*'s crime editor.

Clewes quickly cut a deal and passed him to a copy-taker. 'Anyone coming on the scene would think Elizabeth Yatman, 19, was a victim or a witness...'

He dictated a 300 word front-page story off the top of his head. He felt a buzz of non-chemical high as he compressed the horror into ready-formatted prose..

'What about pictures?' Clewes asked.

Scobie had that covered. 'I could ask multiple k for a pic, but I want your word you'll let me stay on the story. I won't let you down.'

'People don't let me down,' Clewes said. 'People don't let *Derek* down.'

'A pic will be wired.'

Scobie hung up and called the *Herald*. He got Gemma, the two-day a week picture editor, and asked her to look out the shots of Elizabeth (overexposed in a blinding white uniform) taken for the aborted lice feature and wire them to the number Clewes had given him. Gemma chuckled at the mystery but did not ask what was going on.

If Scobie stayed on this bronco, everything would change.

Within a day, he was no longer the only reporter on Elizabeth Yatman. But he was first. The *Comet* broke the story – 'SISTER OF MURDER: INNOCENT FACE OF MONSTER NURSE' – and Elizabeth's now-chilling perky smile was plastered over thirty million newspapers.

The hordes of New Grub Street descended on the West like a New Age convoy, booking every hotel room in Somerset, pestering every Ash Grove pupil, parent and teacher. There was little new stuff to pick over, so everyone dug for background.

No one had suspected anything. She seemed such a nice girl. There was no explanation.

Because he could afford to be generous, Scobie acted as a native guide to the nationals, telling them which pubs to haunt. His exclusive with Greg Dunphy was enough to get him another *Comet* front page.

On the third day, he remembered to call Harry and resign.

Evidence suggested Crispin Toomey, 13, had reported to Elizabeth Yatman with a twisted ankle after a morning break soccer game. The nurse offered to drive him home. Instead, she took him to an unknown location (her car was too clean to have been used) and spent five hours killing him. Then she drove back to town and, sighting a rabbit, had her accident.

Eight other children, aged between eleven and fifteen, were missing. Hitherto, it was presumed they had run away to join the travellers. All but one were pupils at Ash Grove. Four of them, it turned out, were last seen on their way to the nurse for minor treatment. Elizabeth did not say anything about the missing children. It was assumed they were dead, but Scobie wrote a story about the search, holding out the slim hope they might show up alive. It was as well to leaven horror with hope. Scobie had an instinctive understanding of that. Clewes commended him for it and looked forward to meeting him when he relocated to London and took his job on the *Comet*.

This was the most exciting time of his life.

The Monster's parents were dead. The only thing resembling a boy-friend who had turned up was Toby Combs, a shocked youth who helped her cater school outings. There was a much-reprinted photograph, taken at a Hallowe'en social, of Toby and Elizabeth dressed as witches, doling out punch from a bowl labelled with crossbones and the word 'POISON'.

On the fifth day, with Elizabeth still not talking, the *Comet* ran a story about an adulterous pop star on its front page. A sidebar promised more inside on the Monster Nurse, but Scobie had only been able to secure and sell interviews with a former Head who remembered Elizabeth as a pupil at Ash Grove. It turned out she had been a Girl Guide. Harry financed a holiday to Majorca selling file photos of her accepting a Life-Saving Award from a *Blue Peter* presenter.

Scobie felt betrayed. Looking at the star, caught in a flash glare with the sort of microskirted blonde Scobie hoped to associate with when he moved to London, he was panic-stricken. What if tomorrow's *Comet* didn't even have a sidebar?

The first reporters had already drifted back to Bristol and London. The story was still big – television news always put it just after the big international events – but it dwindled daily.

He worried that his horse might be ready to throw him.

Dunphy met him for a pint. Though he had taken a mighty bollocking from Sloman for calling Scobie in the first place, he *was* the copper who caught the killer, even if by accident. Dunphy just about realised what Scobie had known from the first, that getting off his bike to check that Honda in the ditch was the most important thing he'd do in his entire life.

'This is the medical report,' Dunphy said, pulling a folder out of his anorak. 'I did a photocopy.'

Scobie looked down the report. Naturally, Elizabeth was put through an exhaustive series of tests. Her skull was X-rayed in the hope of finding a tumour that might 'explain' her behavioural lapses.

He skimmed a lot of technical detail and hit on something.

'I have a call to make,' he said.

The next day's *Comet* front page carried his story. VIOLENT VIRGIN: MONSTER NURSE HAS NEVER HAD IT.

Heavily-coated policemen spread out in a straggly line and waded across the soggy moor, looking for freshly-turned sod. Grey sky threatened drizzle.

The man from the Mirror complemented Scobie on his 'Violent Virgin' piece. Now, all the other press – even the BBC – called Elizabeth the 'Virgin Monster Nurse'.

'Do you think they'll find anything?' Scobie asked the older journo, a Welshman with a nose raspberried by too many whiskies.

'Let's hope not. This is good for another month. Better than an escaped puma or a little girl down a well.'

'What makes this happen?'

'It's in the air? In the '70s, violent crime – rapes, murders, muggings – rose by ten percent every year. In the '80s, it was 23 percent. Now, it's 31. It's like a bug in society, a 'flu going round. People just catch it and go out and … kill.'

'Is that going to be the angle you write up?'

The journo laughed. 'Lord, no. Punters don't want blather about philosophical illnesses. They want something to blame. It's usually in the water. Maybe Satanic Heavy Metal.'

Elizabeth's CD collection was small and conventional: Andrew Lloyd Webber musicals, light classics used in TV adverts, Take That. Nobody could claim owning both the Broadway and West End cast recordings of *Cats* drove them to kill nine children.

It seemed the line of police had found something, but it was just an old bucket lodged in a ditch.

'Is there a nasties connection?' Clewes asked.

Scobie had thought of that.

'Elizabeth doesn't have a video.'

'Pity. What about the boy-friend?'

Talking on the phone, he imagined the editor pacing his bustling office, sleeves rolled up, minions approaching with proofs and urgent messages.

Scobie tried to remember Toby Combs' front room. The youth had refused to talk with him since the Violent Virgin headline. He wondered if being branded a monster's boy-friend was worse than the revelation that he hadn't even had sex with her.

'Her boy-friend has a video,' Scobie said. 'I'm sure of it.'

'Well, find out if they watched nasties. Or porn. Or anything.'

Scobie imagined Toby and Elizabeth sitting demurely at either end of the sofa watching *Lassie Come Home*. Maybe holding hands during the sad bits.

'It's all on the computer,' Mrs Morris told him. 'I can tell you exactly what any member has rented out. The figures go into a pile at the head office and make up the charts.'

Mrs Morris's shop used to be called Valerie's Videos. Now it was part of a big chain. The place looked like a fast-food outlet, with cassettes instead of burgers.

The charts were propped up on the counter. This week at Number One was *Where the Bodies Are Buried 3*. A poster for the horror film trumpeted its 3-D trip to Hell. Special glasses were provided with each rental.

'Could you tell me what Toby Combs has rented?'

'If I can work this menu properly,' Mrs Morris said, stabbing keys. 'Ah, victory.'

A sheet of paper printed out.

'He's not a very regular renter. Less than one a month.'

Scobie read the list. The only real surprise was the *Comet Knock-Outs Bouncing Beachballs Bonanza*, which featured the topless girls who appeared on the inside pages of the *Comet* playing volleyball in slow motion. Scobie wondered if Toby had asked Elizabeth around that evening, and imagined the youth's violet blushes.

Otherwise, it was all mainstream: *Problem Child, Blame It on the Bellboy, Cocoon, Top Gun, The Little Mermaid*. At the bottom of the list was another title that didn't quite fit: *Where the Bodies Are Buried 3*.

'Did he really take this out?'

Behind the counter towered a cardboard cut-out of Rob Hackwill, the monster from the *Where the Bodies Are Buried* films, single eye flashing red, silver-foiled claws glinting.

'It's a huge rental. We stock copies in depth. Everybody has taken it out. Kids love horror films. I prefer musicals myself.'

'Why would anyone want to pay to be horrified?'

'Have you got a girlfriend? Couples like these films because they're an excuse to cuddle during the scary scenes.'

Scobie imagined Toby putting on *Where the Bodies Are Buried 3* and edging nearer Elizabeth's end of the sofa, arm creeping along cushions behind her back, itching to pounce like Rob Hackwill on a cheerleader. He saw the reflection of the monster in Elizabeth's wide blue eyes.

The *Comet* headline read: TWO FACES OF EVIL. Below were the familiar shot of a smiling Elizabeth in her nurse's hat and a still of the fang-baring monster from one of the *Where the Bodies Are Buried* films. In the article, Scobie asked if *Where the Bodies Are Buried 3* had snapped Elizabeth Yatman's mind, if she had asked Rob Hackwill into her life, if she had acted on orders from the Hollywood bogeyman? He asked the questions: thirty-three million *Comet* readers answered with a series of decisive 'yeses'.

That night, Cloud 9, the satellite channel owned by Derek Leech, the *Comet*'s proprietor, cancelled the *première* of a comedy action film called *Surfin' CIA* to broadcast *Where the Bodies Are Buried 3*. After the transmission, which drew the highest rating of the year, viewers voted by calling one of two numbers: one for those who felt the film definitely caused Elizabeth Yatman's crimes and should be withdrawn, one for those who believed violent films had no effect on society. Leech promised to abide by the results: when 78% of calls said no to Rob Hackwill, he withdrew *Where the Bodies Are Buried 3* from Cloud 9 and promised never to show it again, or any of the other films in the series. At least, not after the Cloud 9 Halloween Midnight-'til-Dawn marathon advertised as 'the last chance to see' all five *Where the Bodies Are Buried* films. The marathon, which followed a news special on the Yatman case, also drew record ratings.

On the suggestion of the *Comet*, video shops reluctantly pulled *Where the Bodies Are Buried 3* off the shelves – since Scobie's story, it was the most popular title in the horror section – and tried to return them to the distributor. When the company wouldn't buy back the tapes, the *Comet* quietly bought a job lot and organised parents' groups and moral crusaders into a mass burning on the rec ground where Elizabeth's victims had once played football. The family of Crispin Toomey were too stricken to attend, but several parents of still-missing children showed up and were photographed throwing cassettes into the flame. Faces contorted, either with loathing or in the natural expression of someone who has inhaled a lungful of burning videotape.

Cloud 9 interviewed Scobie at the burning. He was beginning to wonder whether his future was in print journalism after all. Maybe he could vault from the *Comet* into television.

'These evil films must be stopped,' Scobie said, sincerely. 'How long can we afford to pour filth into weak minds and not expect them to become clogged with insanity?'

Some bystanders cheered him. He was already a local celebrity. Soon he would be a national figure.

The next day, Sloman turned up at his flat, swallowing his dislike. Elizabeth Yatman wanted to see him. She had something to say she would only say to him.

He was alone with the Monster. A matron who resembled Dolph Lundgren was just outside the door, beyond a peephole. Elizabeth's prison dress looked like a dyed-blue nurse's uniform. Anything she wore looked like a nurse's uniform.

'You've made me famous, Mr Scobie. Thank you.'

'You made yourself famous, Elizabeth.'

'I never miss the *Comet*. When I were little, I wanted to be a *Comet* Knock-Out. I didn't grow the chest for it.'

If she posed nude now, she could command a bigger fee than Princess Di. People would be interested.

Scobie did not know what to ask. Asked thousands of questions in the past weeks, she had kept her secrets. In person, she was even more ordinary than in the pictures that had to be doctored to make her eyes shine like evil neon. Her blonde eyebrows were almost invisible.

'Do you watch horror films?'

Elizabeth made a face. 'I get scared. I saw half of *Carry On Screaming* on the telly box once and had nightmares for months.'

'Do you remember *Where the Bodies Are Buried 3*?'

'The film Toby rented?'

'Yes.'

'I read about it in the *Comet*. Sounds horrid.'

'Did you see it?'

She didn't say anything. To the *Herald*, Toby claimed he had been given the film by mistake. He had wanted to rent *When the Whales Came*. None of the nationals picked up that twist on the story.

'Did Rob Hackwill, the monster, make you do... the things you did?'

Elizabeth smiled. 'If it helps the *Comet*, Mr Scobie.'

For the first time, he found her frightening.

'I've a tape of the film, Elizabeth. I've been watching it. Trying to understand.'

'I hope you don't watch it on your own. You'll scare yourself to death.'

It was just a silly horror film. A rubber monster leaping out of the dark, drawing lines of ketchup on aerobicised teenage bodies. Loud noises and bad music. Explosive death and bad jokes. Pathetic.

'There hasn't been so much in the *Comet* lately.'

Elizabeth was off the front page. The search for the missing children had gone on too long to be interesting. Psychiatrists gave interviews with too many polysyllables to be usable.

'It's all Baby Milena and Barry Gatlin.'

Baby Milena was a Bosnian orphan flown to London at Derek Leech's expense for plastic surgery on her badly-burned face. Barry Gatlin was an American comedian who got into a shoot-out with the Los Angeles police after a traffic offence.

'I'd like to help the *Comet*, Mr Scobie. I'd like to tell you where to find...'

She giggled like a 13-year-old.

'Let me put it this way,' she adopted a gruff American movie trailer horror voice, 'I'd like to tell you *Where the Bodies Are Buried...*'

If he didn't tell the police, he could get into trouble. But if he told the police, he'd have to share. He thought of a way of telling the police and keeping his exclusive.

He called Greg Dunphy.

The constable met him for a lunchtime drink at the Valiant Soldier, a pub in Alder. The village was nine miles outside town. Dunphy returned one of the *Comet*'s copies of *Where the Bodies Are Buried 3* to him.

'Couldn't get through it,' he admitted. 'Jimmy and Mandy loved it, though. Horror don't bother them.'

Dunphy's kids went to Ash Grove. Jimmy was in the football team with Crispin Toomey.

Scobie slipped the video into his coat pocket.

'She told me where she did it.'

'Christ!'

'The kids are still there, she says.'

'Christ oh Christ!'

'You and me, we'll beat the detectives from Bristol. We'll find the place. I'll write it up as if we worked out the clues. I'll say she dropped hints.'

Dunphy gulped his pint.

Elizabeth's parents had run a small farm in Alder. With the recession, they'd been badly behind on the mortgage payments when they died in a car crash. Now the bank had the place up for sale. Even with the notoriety of being the childhood home of the Monster Nurse, the farm wasn't shifting.

'The Bristol CID boys were all over,' Dunphy said.

'Elizabeth had a secret den.'

'We dug bloody holes everywhere.'

'It's not under the ground.'

They dragged open the gate and walked up the muddy track towards the house and a barn.

'I should call Sloman.'

'Let's make sure Elizabeth isn't playing us for twazzocks first. Mass murderers have been known to lie.'

The barn-door was open. They went inside. Bare, the barn still smelled of hay and dung. Scobie looked up at the flat wooden roof. Outside, the roof was corrugated iron and curved.

He searched for the rope Elizabeth had told him about.

'Bingo.'

It was wound around a skewer in the ground. Anyone not in the know would assume it was just part of the webbing hay bales were to be fixed to. He untied the rope and gave a strong tug. A trapdoor creaked upwards and a rope ladder fell on Dunphy. The constable yelped and cringed.

'Magic,' Scobie said.

A nasty smell seeped out of the cavity in the roof. He knew the next minutes would be unpleasant.

'Did you bring a torch?' he asked.

'On my bike?'

Scobie fished out his cigarette lighter and made flame. 'This will have to do.'

'You're going up there?'

'Tell you what, you call Sloman.'

Scobie checked the flash on his camera. He would get his own pictures. Exclusive. Official. VIRGIN MONSTER NURSE'S HORROR LAIR.

Dunphy backed away, towards the barn-door. Afternoon light spilled around him. Scobie climbed up to the darkness. He lifted his lighter in through the trapdoor and poked his head into Elizabeth's hidey-hole.

Stench flailed about his face like a chain.

His hand brushed something stiff and crinkly on the surface but soft, moist and giving underneath. He nearly lost his footing on the ladder. A small face, as twisted as anything in *Where the Bodies Are Buried 3*, was close to his own. His flickering lighter gave its shadow-etched features movement. He pulled himself into the low space. There was a gap of about four feet between the wooden floor and the tin ceiling.

How had Elizabeth had convinced the kids to climb the ladder? For the younger ones, it might have been a game. For the older ones, the boys at least, it might have been a promise.

His head spun as he sat in the hidey-hole, surrounded by dead kids. A paraffin lamp stood by the trapdoor. The lighter burned his fingers. Maybe seeing it properly would be better than imagining it from outlines. He lit the lamp and turned up the wick.

Every inch of the hole – tin roof, stone walls, the wooden beams – was collaged with paper. The black and white wasn't red all over, but it was speckled with dark brown that must have been red when fresh. Elizabeth had cocooned herself with newspaper cuttings. *Comet* Knock-Outs, interchangeable breasts and smiles, were plastered throughout news pictures and headlines. From the Knock-Outs' hairstyles, Scobie knew Elizabeth had been papering this den since the early '80s, since before she was ten years old.

There were famous headlines. GERTCHA GOUCHOS!, from the Falklands War. HANG HUSSEIN!, from the Gulf War. DID ELVIS DIE OF AIDS?: OUR PSYCHIC REVEALS THE TRUTH. HAIRY PASSAGE: HAMSTER IN HOLLYWOOD HUNK'S BACK ENTRANCE. BUGGER OFF, BRUSSELS! PAY YOUR POLL TAX AND WIN A FORD MONTEGO. A run-down of Derek Leech's evolving political position: MAGGIE WALLOPS KINNOCK, MAGGIE RULES, MAGGIE MUST STAY, MAGGIE MUST GO, MAJOR WALLOPS KINNOCK, MAJOR RULES, MAJOR MUST STAY, MAJOR MUST GO. Wars, football, riots, bingo. Royal Romances, Royal Weddings, Royal Divorces. Strikes, scandals, silly season dog-biting, sex, soap, satellite TV.

All the cuttings were from the *Comet*.

Myra Hindley, Peter Sutcliffe, Dennis Nilsen, Jack the Ripper, the Krays, the Black Panther, Ted Bundy, Jeffrey Dahmer, David Koresh, Ivan the Terrible, Frederick West. Murderers and criminals stared out of dozens of *Comet* front pages. Headlines spoke of Monster Manors, Horror Houses, Axe Atrocities, Gun Sieges, Terror Lairs, Human Fiends, Pitiless Gazes, Killer Smiles, Death Cars, Satin Satans.

When she was little, Elizabeth Yatman wanted to get into the *Comet* by posing topless, but she didn't grow the chest for it. She'd found another way to get her wish.

This was not a story which would sell.

With decisive certainty, Scobie plucked clippings from surfaces where they had been gummed. The old paper tore and crumbled.

He stayed away from the corpses as he ripped. A mossy clump of Knock-Out pin-ups, moulded together by damp, came off in a great rip. Stabs of daylight came through joins between the tin sheets of the roof. The space was small enough to be cleared completely in enough time. He would be done before Dunphy got back with Sloman.

He scrunched the clippings into a ball the size of a pillow and dropped it through the trapdoor. The ball came apart on the bare earth floor of the barn. He could easily scoop it together and get it to the car. It would all burn later.

A last look-around showed him he had done a good job. Nothing remained of Elizabeth's tabloid collage.

One more touch. He took the *Where the Bodies Are Buried 3* video out of his pocket and propped it against a beam. Rob Hackwill's rubber snarl caught his eye. The monster, framed on the cover, seemed to be swearing vengeance.

The next day's *Comet* headline was obvious: MONSTER NURSE: WHERE THE BODIES WERE BURIED.

Elizabeth's lawyers started bleating about the evil influences of Rob Hackwill. In Hollywood, Allan Keyes, English creator of *Where the Bodies Are Buried*, had no comment. Snordlij Svensson, the Icelandic movie brat who directed *Where the Bodies Are Buried 3*, was too busy on *Cretaceous Cop*, the hundred million dollar summer blockbuster he had landed on the strength of his work on the horror sequel, to say anything quotable.

Cloud 9 staged a debate about the effects of horror violence on impressionable minds, between Morag Duff, a right-wing Labour MP and 'moral crusader', and Shelley Carlisle, a film critic who edited *Rabid*, the 'International Magazine of Cine-Terror'. Scobie, plugged into the information super-highway, chaired the show.

'I think the pressure should be on those who claim film violence *doesn't* have an effect to prove their case,' said the politician. 'Lives are at stake. It seems strange to plead freedom of speech when kids are being killed. If one life is saved, surely it's worth getting rid of a load of pernicious rubbish.'

The studio audience agreed with her. Someone got up and said 'even if horror films don't cause real horror, we can do without them. Let's ban the bastards to be on the safe side.'

Shelley Carlisle, who was quite attractive in a Goth sort of way, looked disgusted and got flustered. She tried to make a point but he cut in.

'Shelley,' he began, heavily, 'if you'd been in that barn, you'd never be able to watch a horror film again.'

*

On the first day of the trial, the judge commented he thought it 'quite likely' Elizabeth had been influenced by *Where the Bodies Are Buried 3*. In the *Comet*, Scobie wrote 'JUDGE BLAMES NASTY: OFFICIAL'.

The next day, Valerie's Video, which had binned its entire stock of horror films, was broken into by vandal vigilantes who piled cassettes of animal comedies on the floor and set a fire. Mrs Morris, who lived in a flat upstairs, was stricken by smoke inhalation but rescued in time to survive. The *Comet* called her 'another victim of the curse of Rob Hackwill'.

In parliament, Morag Duff called for a crack-down on 'horror books and videos' and received cross-party support for a bill which would bring in stringent new regulations. The British Board of Film Classification withheld certificates from films by Wes Craven, Quentin Tarantino and Martin Scorsese. Johnny Faith, an unemployed fitter caught while holding up his fifth post office, claimed he was ordered to a life of crime by Rob Hackwill. Madame Tussaud's Chamber of Horrors and the London Dungeon were picketed by the Concerned Parents' Group. Scobie and Morag Duff addressed the CPG rally.

'Christmas With Frank and Drac', a holiday season of Hammer Films, was announced by BBC1, then pulled after a wave of public protest. A chain of newsagent's, one of Derek Leech's holdings, refused to stock *Rabid*, which ceased publication. Libraries took books by Shaun Hutson, Allan Keyes and James Herbert off their shelves, lending them by written request only to those who could prove they were over eighteen. Publishers rejacketed the backlists of Stephen King and Clive Barker, tagging the authors as 'the master of dark suspense' and 'the prince of *fiction magique*'. Cloud 9 broadcast *Apocalypse Now* with the swearing and violence left in, but the line 'the horror ... the horror' removed from the soundtrack.

Peter Paul Patrick, a convicted arsonist, set off a fire bomb in a private club where old horror films were shown. Five people died in reel two of the 1943 *Henry Aldrich Haunts a House*. Patrick claimed it was time 'to rid the world of Rob Hackwill and the perverts who are his disciples'. 57% of *Comet* readers agreed with him.

Throughout her trial, Elizabeth Yatman was polite but said very little. She never exactly claimed to have been influenced by, or even seen, *Where the Bodies Are Buried 3*, but she didn't deny it either. Her lawyers argued she was driven by the phantasm of Rob Hackwill, and that she should not be blamed for her actions. She was committed to Broadmoor, presumably for the rest of her life. In his summing-up, the Judge reiterated his remarks about the *Where the Bodies Are Buried* films. The Prime Minister promised action.

He was too busy to settle properly into his new flat, so everything sat in boxes. Scobie was earning more in a month on the *Comet* than he had in a year on the *Herald*. Harry and Gemma and other Backwater bods clubbed together and bought him a big dictionary as a leaving present. He had used it once, while deciding whether to label a Cabinet Minister a 'pedophile' or a 'paedophile'. In the end, a sub altered it to 'child molester'.

He started going out with Lizzie Trilling, who had come second in the Knock-Out of the Year contest. Her breasts were strange, like giant haemorrhoids. She had no feeling at all in her nipples. When she told him she had originally wanted to be a nurse, he lost an erection.

Clewes used him only for major stories: the private indiscretions of public figures, and violent crime. As the *Comet* spokesman in the campaign against horror, Scobie became a public figure himself. Some journos even started sniffing around his private life, but the *Comet* – which had unusual resources – frightened them off.

When a drugs war broke out in a North London estate, Scobie was the first reporter on the scene. In a flack jacket, he dragged a photographer through small-arms fire.

'This way, Mr Scobie,' said the deferential police sergeant. The *Comet* was very law and order. A lot of policemen read it. 'We've cleared out the trouble-makers.'

The house had iron shutters over the windows. The door was kicked in. An armoured policeman stood guard like a knight outside a castle. Scobie noticed bullet-pocks in the stone cladding.

'This was the field headquarters of the zonk gang.'

Zonk, a new cocaine derivative, was just filtering through into the British market. Competition between dealers was leading to many skirmishes.

Scobie stepped over the welcome mat. The hallway was still smoky. There were blood-squirts on the flock wallpaper. The fitted stair carpets had been raked with gunfire.

The photographer took pictures of Scobie striding around.

'This was their command centre,' the sergeant said, indicating the lounge.

'It's a bit of a mess.'

There were corpse outlines on the lino. Blood spattered on a scrunched carpet of newspapers, all recent editions of the *Comet*. Elizabeth smiled from several of his front page stories. The room was full of expensive equipment: computers, a fax, a HDTV screen, a video. Stapled to the walls were *Comet* Knock-Outs. Lizzie's full lips, as siliconed as her chest, kiss-mouthed off half a dozen full-colour shots.

'What's in the video?' he asked.

A policeman tried to press buttons with thick-gloved fingers. A tape ejected.

'Something nasty, I'll bet,' the sergeant said.

The policeman looked at the spine and read '*The* Comet *Official History of the Gulf War.*'

'Taking tips on bombing, I'll be bound.'

The sergeant opened his crime scene briefcase and pulled out a cassette.

'Shove this in, sonny. The chief likes it tidy.'

The sergeant handed his man a copy of *Where the Bodies Are Buried 3* and gave Scobie the wink.

'Has to be an explanation for all this crime and violence, eh?'

Unable to drift off, Scobie left Lizzie open-mouthed on her back – for her, there wasn't any other way to sleep – and padded into his bare front room. He didn't have any chairs yet, but the Home Entertainment System was fully installed. It was a present from Derek Leech, a perk of the new job. He sat on the carpet and watched *Where the Bodies Are Buried 3*. He still had several copies left.

Know Your Enemy, he thought.

Every time he watched the film, it was a different. It must be an illusion. Some scenes he remembered being subtle were explicit. Some actors faces changed. The tapes were like siblings, alike but not identical. Each copy had its own peculiarities.

This was the Tiffany Tape. The scene with Tiffany, Hackwill's first victim, having sex with her boy-friend before he turns into the monster, was minutes longer and more graphic than in any of his other copies. Tiffany was a nurse. In sex-play, her boyfriend mapped her pleasure centres with acupuncture needles. Hackwill turned them into syringes and filled her with hellfire. She expanded with pleasure, veins popping all over her nude body, and exploded in orgasm.

Scobie found the Tiffany Tape more disturbing than other variations: the Adam Kiss Tape (more talk scenes), the Raving Rob Tape (more screaming monster) and the Loud Shit Tape (more heavy metal). He watched it more often.

Tiffany looked a little like Elizabeth Yatman. Almost all women, and some men, looked a little like Elizabeth.

If Morag Duff's unopposed Private Member's Bill passed, Scobie would be liable to pay a £50 fine for every tape of *Where the Bodies Are Buried 3* he owned. He thought of disposing of them, but that might leave him in the dark, unprotected. As long as he kept looking at *Where the Bodies Are Buried 3*, Rob Hackwill was prevented from looking at him.

He frame-advanced through Tiffany's death scene, trying to discern the movie magic used to make her die.

Real Press, Derek Leech's publishing firm, signed him to do a quickie book on the Monster Nurse and the Evil Effects of Horror Videos. It would be called, of course, *Where the Bodies Were Buried*. Letters of support poured in from the CPG and ordinary citizens. Morag Duff, who agreed to write a preface to the book, took him and Lizzie out to dinner at Langan's and gave him sound-bites all evening. Everything she said was strident and quotable.

Fifth generation copies of any of the *Where the Bodies Are Buried* films changed hands on the black market for up to £500. Customs reported they seized more Dutch-subtitled horror movies than porn. Peter Paul Patrick was remanded into psychiatric care. Scobie discovered Patrick was the survivor of child abuse and that the grandparents who had tormented him in childhood were both lookalikes, at least in photographs, for Boris Karloff.

Scobie knew *Where the Bodies Are Buried 3* so well he could dream it, with endless variations. Sometimes he was Adam Kiss, the journalist hero tormented by the ghost of the murderer he had written about. Sometimes he was Rob Hackwill, clacking claws as he sought revenge. Sometimes, Tiffany was Lizzie, every part of her body but her breasts rippling during the sex scenes. Sometimes, Tiffany was Elizabeth, filling hypos from a punch-bowl marked 'POISON'.

At the office, Clewes handed him an envelope. 'A letter from your girl-friend.'

It was a note from Elizabeth, offering to help with his book. She was looking forward to reading more about herself. Scobie showed it to Clewes.

'Publicity junkie. That's why she let herself get caught.'

Scobie wasn't sure it was that simple.

'Think about it. She left eight kids in the loft where she killed them but drove into a ditch with Crispin in the passenger seat. Why didn't she leave him with the others?'

'I don't get it.'

'It had gone on too long. She wasn't enjoying anonymity. She didn't even enjoy killing the little brats. She was waiting for you to come along and make her famous.'

'It didn't have to be me.'

Clewes shrugged. 'No, but you're her Dr Watson, her Boswell. She's as much a creature of the *Comet* as Lizzie Trilling or Princess Di or Morag Duff. Or me.'

In the office, Scobie was called 'Monster Hunter'. The nickname stuck and was used by his police contacts.

'You'll need a strong tummy for this, MH,' said Detective Inspector Hollis. 'It's carnage on a carpet.'

They were on a staircase in a Soho walk-up, outside a flat used as a place of business by a young woman who called herself 'Ariane'. Her real name was June Lowther.

The DI pushed the open door. The familiar stench hit Scobie. Death always smelled like Elizabeth's barn loft.

'Hacked up like a jigsaw.'

This was the third. Like the others, Ariane was a prostitute, but not a streetwalker. No card downstairs offered 'busty model' or 'Miss Strict'. Her clients had to know her address. Her murderer was probably one of them.

Theresa Gottschalk, the first victim, called herself 'Tiffany'. That set wheels in motion. The story Scobie wrote about the Gottschalk murder was headlined 'DOES A REAL ROB HACKWILL STALK LONDON TARTS?' He expected the second victim to be a Nancy, like Hackwill's second victim in *Where the Bodies Are Buried 3*, but she was called Muriel Bone. Nevertheless, the connection was made in the public mind. All coverage of the crimes called the unknown murderer 'the real Rob

Hackwill'.

Scobie stepped carefully around Ariane, who was cut up and spread out on the floor. A polythene sheet was laid over her, but splotches of blood showed where it pressed an open wound. A black rag of hair was like a pond plant trapped under ice.

'This Hackwill is one sick puppy,' said Hollis.

'It's the same man?' Scobie asked.

'Left his calling card.'

Stuck to a mirror with bloodspots was a *Comet* Knock-Out. It wasn't Lizzie, but might have been. The killer had biroed dotted lines across the smiling pin-up's body. He might as well have inked in little scissors with 'cut here' instructions.

At the Tiffany crime scene, it *had* been a picture of Lizzie.

With tweezers, Hollis removed the Knock-Out and slipped the page into a clear plastic envelope. The police agreed with Scobie that this detail be kept back from the official press releases, so copycat crimes could be excluded from the investigation.

'Any luck on a little black book?'

Searches of the other victims' flats had not turned up any sort of address book or client list. The assumption was that the killer took away anything that might give away his name.

'Our laddie likes the ladies,' said Hollis. 'You should have him judge the Knock-Out of the Year Contest.'

A rasping came from the flat's tiny kitchen. Scobie and Hollis jumped.

Stacy Cotterill pushed through the bead curtain. The Detective Constable looked too young to get into an 18 certificate film.

'She had a computer, sir,' Cotterill said. 'I found a file named KISSES. It's printing out names and addresses.'

Hollis grinned. 'Just like Crippen. Caught because he didn't keep up with new technology.'

'The list is annotated, sir. Explicitly.'

The DI looked down at Ariane. 'Who's a clever girl, then?'

As Clewes finished his speech, Scobie and Hollis stood at the back of the room. They were near the apex of the Derek Leech Enterprises Pyramid in London Docklands. Clewes was addressing a seminar on the marketing of the *Comet*, which Leech wanted replicated throughout his media empire.

'The *Comet* was a dead duck when Derek bought it out,' Clewes said. 'It was the most boring tabloid in Britain. It was more boring than most of the heavies...'

There was dutiful laughter from the suits.

Ariane's client list included a few familiar names: Alistair Garnett, a high-ranking civil servant who helped draft Morag Duff's anti-horror bill, liked 'the usual' but always 'got it over with quickly'. Scobie was surprised to discover Morag herself couldn't 'get enough fist' and 'needs it up to the elbow'. None of these were real Rob Hackwill suspects. An assortment of alibis, unearthed in embarrassing interviews, checked out.

Among a lot of anonymous suits whose performance rated demeaning remarks, the only one who seemed a likely prospect was Ronald Clewes. Ariane noted he got 'rough, then weepy'.

DI Hollis asked Scobie to smooth the way. Scobie was well aware how difficult this would be to write up. No blame must attach to the *Comet*. But Ronald Clewes *was* the *Comet*. He was Derek Leech's blue-eyed editor. He had risen from the subs pits on the strength of 'GERTCHA GAUCHOS'.

'Derek thought of the Knock-Outs,' Clewes continued. 'Derek thought of everything. In the '70s, circulation rose an average of ten per cent each year after Derek became proprietor. In the '80s, it was 23 percent. In the '90s, 31.'

The figures were creepily familiar.

In a shadowed corner stood a tall figure, himself shadowed. Scobie somehow thought it might be Derek Leech, whom he had never met face to face, but he was turned away, unrecognisable. Unusually, he wore a black slouch hat indoors, and a long black coat.

Clewes stood before a panoramic window which was turned to mirror by nightfall. His reflection mimicked his gestures. The reflection looked like Rob Hackwill. Scobie knew his boss was the murderer.

Cotterill sidled in and leaned close to Hollis.

'We've been through his desk, sir,' she said, nodding at Clewes. 'He kept *souvenirs*.'

Hollis made a face.

Polite applause concluded the seminar. The suits left. Clewes looked at Scobie and the detectives. The shadowman was still there, watching.

'Ronald...' Scobie began.

Clewes turned and looked at his face in the window mirror. It contorted, teeth bared, eyes red.

'He's Hackwill,' Hollis said.

Clewes head-butted the window. It cracked across and night-wind whistled through.

Hollis waded through chairs. Scobie just watched. Clewes launched himself through the window.

Officially, the real Rob Hackwill was still at large. Leech cut a deal with Hollis. Since his divorce, Clewes had filled his house with contact sheets from the Knock-Out shoots. He must have obsessed about the girls for years.

Lizzie wasn't around much. She got a part as a tart in a film about Jack the Ripper, but production was shut down when the video distributors, afraid of the 'horror' tag, pulled out their money. She settled instead for a *Comet* Knock-Out tape called *Wet Melons*. It wasn't the same.

At every crime scene he visited, Scobie found the *Comet*. Used to wrap fish 'n' chips. A headline pasted to a wall. A face or a pair of breasts cut out of a picture. The Royal Divorce colour pull-out special. The police tidily disposed of the evidence, always leaving a cassette of one of the Where the Bodies Are Buried films in place of the newspaper.

The tapes were getting quite rare. His own stash was dwindling: the machine ate the Adam Kiss Tape, he had to give the Loud Shit Tape to Hollis to leave under the dangling feet of a teenage suicide. He mainly watched the Tiffany Tape.

He felt as close to Rob Hackwill as to a brother.

The week the *Comet* reacted to an EU scare about BSE with a series of recipes making use of 'Best British Beef', Scobie received a food parcel from Broadmoor. Elizabeth sent him a *Comet*-approved 'cow pie' she had made herself. In her note, she asked how the book was coming on.

He sat and stared at the pie, wondering.

In the month after Morag (Glove Puppet) Duff's Private Member's Bill became law, there were mass burnings of horror videos, books, comics and magazines in all major British cities. The editors of a series of paperback original horror anthologies were convicted under the Duff Law and served three weeks in prison. A bespectacled writer, hailed as the leading light of the 'miserabilist' horror movement, chained himself to railings outside the Houses of Parliament and was pelted with rubbish by a mob. The police staged a series of dawn raids on the homes of horror book and video collectors, parading sorry culprits before their neighbours as quantities of material were shovelled out of their houses.

While covering the ongoing campaign against horror, the *Comet*'s circulation rose by 44% As zonk became the drug of choice for the unemployed and Rob Hackwill imitators committed strings of murders in Cardiff and Manchester, violent crime also rose by 44%.

Scobie began to avoid interview requests. He put on his telephone answering machine and never returned calls from the media.

Every night, he watched the Tiffany Tape. It might be the last copy of *Where the Bodies Are Buried 3* in Great Britain. He knew now that the film was innocent; the Monster lived somewhere nearer.

One night, the film was interrupted by a commercial break which had never been there before.

Two *Comet* Knock-Outs jiggled in bikini bottoms around a seated figure reading the newspaper. The headline read HACKWILL MUST GO. From behind the paper peeped a snarling face. A single red eye winked at Scobie. Rob Hackwill said 'you have to have a giggle, don't you?'

The girls cuddled close to the monster, who stuck his claw-hands into their soft bellies and poked sharp fingers out through their breasts. They bled silicon.

'What's black and white and red all over?' the monster asked. 'A newspaper?'

Hollis didn't say who he was but Scobie recognised the voice.

'Pick up, MH,' he said. 'It's about the Real Rob.'

Scobie took the phone and identified himself.

'Ariane had a copy of her list. It's gone to another paper. They'll make the Clewes connection. Tell Leech I can't cover for the *Comet* this time.'

The policeman hung up.

On the screen, Hackwill stalked Adam Kiss through an intestinal corridor. Scobie knew there wasn't time to get round to Clewes's still-sealed house, dispose of the Knock-Outs and leave the Tiffany Tape. The connection would be made.

It was his own fault. He had embedded in the public mind the notion that violent crime was caused by something in the media. Now horror was gone, something else would take its place.

Something like the *Comet*. The newspaper, a Derek Leech product, had seeped out and touched people: people like Elizabeth, Peter Paul Patrick, Clewes, the zonk gangs.

The phone rang again. Scobie picked up before the answering message could cut in.

'You know who this is,' the voice said. It was deep, almost American. Scobie couldn't be sure whether it was Derek Leech or Rob Hackwill. 'And you know what to do.'

On the screen, Hackwill closed on Adam Kiss, mouth expanding to fasten around his head.

The darkness wasn't in the film. It was in the Docklands Pyramid. Scobie was its servant, just as Elizabeth and Clewes had been its servants. He had no choice about his future.

Scobie rooted through unopened house-warming presents. Clewes had given him just the thing. A cordless electric carving knife. Probably the same model Clewes used himself.

It took half an hour to work out the instructions. The appliance had to be plugged in for three hours before it was powered. It would have been frustrating but he timed the period by playing the Tiffany Tape twice. What he was planning would mean the extinction of the film and its like. He was absent-mindedly sorry for the loss, but the *Comet* must go on.

At a button touch, the blade buzzed. He touched it experimentally to the polystyrene packaging, which flew with a shriek into hundreds of tiny snowballs.

He took out his address book and ordered a Spicy Hawaiian Pizza from a firm that used girls as despatch riders. Then he called an 'oriental masseuse' who gave home service and asked her to come over immediately. He left a message with Lizzie's answering service asking her to call in person as soon as possible to pick up a contract marked 'urgent' which had come from her agent. Then he telephoned DC Cotterill's answering machine and asked if she could come over this evening to do an interview for his book.

That, he decided, was enough. Four possibles.

He sat in the recliner in front of the television, electric knife in one hand, video remote in the other. He gave an experimental buzz into the air, fascinated by the whirring blade, then rewound *Where the Bodies Are Buried 3*. He should watch the Tiffany Tape through at least one last time before any of his callers came.

WHERE THE BODIES
ARE BURIED 2020

Spring Meadow, Illinois. Anytown, U.S.A., in the Middle America of the mind. A night in fall, a full moon.

Chantal, consciousness uneasily nestled within the Tina simile, looked through the viewpoint character's eyes. As Tina, she stood alone in a patch of fenced-in park.

The verdigrised town founder, a crooked politician two centuries gone, posed on a pedestal. The statue was in sharp focus, richly dimensional, palpably solid.

Mimesis was generations beyond Virtual.

Dreamwelt was indistinguishable from Actual, affording complete sensory interface. Through the Tina construct, Chantal heard cicada chirrup on the backtrack; felt crisp cold, to the bone; saw breath clouding in damp whispers; smelled grass, after rain.

The indistinct receptors VR did not connect with were active. Her backbrain was absorbing infobits it would take conscious effort to scroll. A million tiny subliminals supported the dream.

Spring Meadow *tasted* real.

INITIATE TITLE SEQUENCE

Disembodied words ghosted in front of the statue, filling the night with letters of jagged green newsprint.

WHeRE tHE BodiES Are BurlEd

The words came apart like mist. She wasn't sure how to make the dream RUN. She couldn't swivel her neck – 'her' neck – to shift viewpoint.

PAUSE

'Don't try to think what it's *like*, Sister Chantal. Just let it happen.'

Jerome's voice seemed to come from empty air, blotting out all other sound and sense. Merely by giving the advice, he made it impossible for her to take it. Aural bleed-through wavered the dreamwelt, shattering the statue into pixels.

Behind the bead curtain of dreamnight, Chantal saw spectre-shapes. Jerome Rhodes and Roger Duroc were watching over her, monitoring her progress.

What was she doing really? Sitting on the couch or standing like Tina, a puppet jerked along by the program?

She felt the weight of the hoodset, the pull of her regular body, the gravity of realwelt.

The curtain hung still, the statue reformed.

STILL PAUSE

She felt the cold again, and heard insects. The spectres were hidden. Calming, she tried to accept the dream. She recognised that she found it hard to surrender to Mimesis.

People do this for *fun*, she reminded herself. For *entertainment*.

A smart program probed for a way around her mental block. She tried not to feel violated.

Chantal did not trust stories, but they still fascinated her. She was not sure which of her conflicting reactions was wrong.

As Tina, her viewpoint was fixed. It was like – 'don't try to think what it's *like*' – wearing a thick suit of too-tight clothes wired rigid by an armature sewn in the lining. She could feel everything, but do nothing.

Her itch to move her neck affected the dreamscene, shifting the visionfield.

180° PAN

The movement was part of the dream, not of her volition. She saw more of the square. Carefully-trimmed trees. A white-painted bench. Abandoned civic buildings. A black cat – very convincing, lithely alive – slunk through bushes, cringing in moonlight. Something dark wafted across the penny-bright face of the moon.

Atmos, atmos.

Despite blurbclaims, it was not like *being* the viewpoint. Chantal wore Tina's dreambody, but was a *dybbuk*, a passenger in her – its – 'mind'.

She could resist the dream, but impetus was to carry on with the story.

Something gave.

RUN

Under the wind, chords sounded, building, suspenseful. Her heart – hers or Tina's? – pounded faster. That cat was gone, melding with liquid shadows. The moon was clear.

The viewpoint looked around. Not the smooth pan of the last movement, but quick, birdlike darts. The pan was to get the dreamer accustomed to visionfield shifts. This was how people saw realwelt; through a skull-camera mounted on a neck-gyro, blurring transitions between shaky half-hemispheres of SurroundSound CineRama.

Tina was waiting, expectant and a little afraid, for someone. There was to be a meeting at midnight. By the old clock on the town hall – something of a cliché – it was a breath away from twelve.

Tina was maybe fifteen years younger than Chantal, in her late teens. She wondered who the girl was.

The dream reacted: a 'Tina Singleton' packet opened, down-loading infodump. Flash-images of parents and friends, establishing relationships. A rolling scroll of backstory. Facts and figures about Spring Meadow. Blips of childhood, blats of school, blurts of domestic terror. Tina was a good student, popular at Spring Meadow High. Her home life was uncertain, locked between feuding parents. Sometimes, Mom – reversal of expectations – got zonked and hurt her. Dad didn't want to notice.

Technically, Mimesis was impressive. But not real, any more than reading a book or watching a motion picture. It was just a story.

The wind raised a flurry of leaves, which swirled around the statue, drifted against her legs. She snatched an oak leaf, held it up. Through the viewpoint's fingers, it seemed absolutely real. She crunched it up and threw it away.

How much information had she just converted?

The park was deserted. Chantal stubbornly sensed Jerome and Duroc, tuning in from outside dreamwelt. And something else.

Another presence.

Tina's nerves frazzed in fearful anticipé. Chantal was puzzled. This sharing of mindspace was not what she expected. Tentatively, she clicked on Tina, allowing more seep-through.

Tina had been receiving Valentines, collaged of newsprint like blackmail notes. At first, sweet.

THeeNk*ng of U, allwAyS.

Then sinister, intimating secret knowledge.

HoW'S MoMMY's leeTle guRL?

Why didn't this twittette go to her School Confessor? There were so many safety nets.

Of course, Chantal knew why:

This is just a stupid story. Logical behaviour would spoil it.

Today's note:

MEaT ME, ToWN $quAre @ MEEDNiGHT.

Unlike the others, it was signed; in an arachnoidal scrawl:

Rob Hackwill.

The name triggered an eerie melody that rose and fell with the swirl of leaves.

Another information package appeared, sealed for the now. Chantal intuited more backstory.

Rob Hackwill was the villain, the killer, the monster. A blackmailer, tortured to death by his corrupt victims; back from the grave for revenge on hypocrite and innocent alike; an agent of the Devil Princess of Hell, tormented and tormenting; a franchise from the last century, still lurking in the collective pop-unconscious.

While preparing her thesis on the Hackwill Effect, Chantal had seen *Where the Bodies Are Buried*, the original motion picture, over and over. Before that, Hackwill had haunted her childhood nightmares. When her Confessor suggested the academic work was an attempt to deal with earlier terrors, he had not told her anything she had not intuited for herself.

Why did the first wide-release Mimesis production have to be a dremake of *Where the Bodies Are Buried*? Why not *Little Women* or *La Dolce Vita*?

Tina looked around nervoso. She was sure it was all skit. Stacey Snyder, her bestest ammi, projected she was *sooooo* funny. This was muchissimo. There would be payback in school tomorrow.

Or maybe it was Jimmy Traynor. One of the Hackwill notes was about him:

Yr SeeCret's saFE, I KnOW U ♡♡♡♡ JiMMy T.

She had no secret crush on Jimmy. No, she was lying to herself. Tina dezzed desperé that Jimmy would glom her.

Chantal was frustrated. The teenthink was difficult to follow. She tried to take over viewpoint, cutting the slango, communicating danger.

From the back of Tina's cramped mind construct, she shouted: look behind you, run away, go home, pull up the covers, call the cops! She caught herself trying to influence a fictional character. She had not expected to be fooled in quite this way. It was absurd.

Jimmy and Stacey were guilty, Tina was pozz. Stacey had snitched her crush to Jimmy. They were gagging together, in the bushes. Her heart would fraction again. There was no Secret Admirer. That scut was only in bad movies – Hah! – and daydreams. There was no Rob Hackwill.

Hadn't Tina registered the name? Didn't this town remember? There had been a dozen sequels. It was impossible that anyone wouldn't know. After thirteen murder-filled films, Rob Hackwill should be as famous in the storywelt as in the real.

Of course, the Mimesis wasn't so much sequel as remake. According to the blurb, this was supposed to 'reinvent the mythos', to take Hackwill 'back to his festering origins' and make him 'a monster for the new millennium'.

Something barrelled at her. A clawed hand grasped her shoulder. Music leaped like a jaguar. Her throat opened in scream. She was pulled around and knocked down.

Gotcha!

Even *knowing* this would happen did not make it less of a shock.

Pressed into soft grassy earth, she sensed the weight of the dark shape pinning her. She smelled a foul breath. She heard muttering.

'I know... Robbie knows... Robbie has always known ... *where the bodies are buried*!'

Her coat ripped at shoulder-seam, sliced by a razor-edged claw-nail. There was something like pain and something like warmth – few want to be hurt in a dream, though the option's there – as the nail pierced Tina's shoulder.

Why would anyone want to pay for this?

Chantal wanted STOP, but had no control. Tina could not struggle; the monster had her. Chantal was completely sucked in by the viewpoint. There was no Chantal Juillerat, S.J.; only Tina Singleton, doomed girl.

The nail grew in her shoulder-wound, scraping past bone, through ligament. Everything distorted. Pain substitute flooded her mind.

The viewpoint was on her back, looking up. The statue stood above, like a towering gravestone. A face thrust close to her, eclipsing the statue and the moon. Sharp teeth clacked, several centimetres of enamel exposed. A single red eye gleamed.

An ice fist took her heart...

'*The Hack is back!*'

... and squeezed.

STOP EJECT

The dreamwelt vanished like ice on a griddle, but there were after-sensations. Chantal still felt Tina's terror.

She needed a moment to reorient.

She was on the couch, as when she had initiated **RUN**. Physically, she had not moved.

Jerome fussed at the dreamdeck. He had ordered **STOP** – didn't he think she could take it? – and was extracting the dreamsphere from its tray. Eyepieces receded into her hoodset.

It took moments for hearing to return. Her brain had to recalibrate for reality, after only minutes of Mimesis.

'Sister, art thou all right in thyself?' asked Duroc.

She nodded and lifted off the hoodset. She shook her hair out – as if she had Tina's shoulder-length blonde fall rather than her own black bob – and scanned the inside of the contraption. Transparent padding protected a neural network of wires and crystal chips.

The Mimesis Process was, in the end, only light. Dreams reached the brain through the optic nerves, duping neural receptors into interpreting nanoflashes as sight, sound, smell, taste, pain, pleasure. But it was hard to remember the tech when a monster was kissing you to death.

She waved Duroc away and looked a question at Jerome.

'I thought you were losing yourself,' he answered.

'I'd have preferred to make the decision from the inside.'

'You're right, Sister. I'm sorry.'

Both Duroc and Jerome used the archaic form, 'Sister'. At the Euro-Commission press conference in Brussels, she had been required to wear full habit for the cameras. She was embarrassed by the penguin costume, which made her a sexless nonperson. She preferred a plain dark single-piece with a discreet roman collar.

The floor swayed slightly: the ship easing on its moorings, not her strings being snipped. Her spinal spirit level was settling. She had her weltview back. She returned the hoodset to its cradle.

The Eunion Parliament had argued in circles about where to site the Euro-Commission on the Model-Duff Amendment. Brussels had superior facilities, but a policy of positive anti-bias against second-generation members meant they were in Prague.

The influx of Eurocracy with Czechia's two-year chairing of EU put office space at a premium. E-Com wound up with the *Gustav Meyrink*, a riverboat at permanent anchor near the Charles Bridge. Subotai, the Mongol indentured to E-Com as minion, joked that the ship constituted the Bohemian Navy.

Her quarters, one deck down, were not much smaller than her cell in Castel Sant'Angelo. Jerome, unused to the cenobite life, nagged admin into getting him a hotel suite. Duroc seemed not to mind his cabin. He had little baggage.

'Thoughts, Sister?'

Tina haunted her. And the stab of Hackwill's claw was a phantom twinge in her shoulder.

'Not yet, Duroc. This will take time. The tech has outpaced the psych. There'll have to be long-term studies.'

'That's what the Industry says,' put in Jerome. 'But they regard mass audiences as a field test. We've too much gen on Mimesis, not enough cognition.'

Jerome Rhodes was English, an Information Analyst. Chantal was Swiss, a Media Psychologist. Their skills were supposed to be complementary. They had not worked together before E-Com seconded their services.

'Then again, the Industry has been co-operative. Pyramid are allowing us dreams well before the public. *Bodies* hasn't been theatrical in the States, much less cleared for Home Mimesis.'

He was in his late twenties, which gave her a year or so on him. He cultivated a slender boyishness she was not yet pozz – a stray Tina word – suited him. He. might be a template for her in-progress/back-burnered bookfile on Information Children: a global generation whose personality, values and culture were shaped by mediamass rather than religion, family background, social class or nationality.

Something had made him **STOP** and pull her out.

'The Industry wants absolution, Jerome,' she said. 'Just as Model-Duff – offence none, Duroc – want us to condemn Mimesis. Everybody deems it in their interest to co-operate. It gets them to where they cognit they can influence us.'

Pyramid Releasing was part of the Derek Leech Group. The multi-media mogul had offered to underwrite the study, but E-Com could not directly accept credit from a source with such a stake in Mimesis, any more than from lobbyists who wanted the Model-Duff Amendment passed into Euro-Law. Leech had been working towards Mimesis since the turn of the century.

'There is Evil around,' Duroc said. 'The Reverend Model has warned us.'

Roger Duroc was a Hardline Christian Zealot, a French follower of Joseph Model, the Liechtensteinian Euro-Vangelist. A big man in his forties, he was a veteran of the Basque Insurrection of '09. While Jerome wore Oxford bags and a tartan *Gorille* jacket, Duroc dressed like a 19th Century ascetic: black suit fastened with pegs, white shirt pinned at the throat. Like other extreme sects, Modelists abjured buttons.

With Britain's Prime Minister Morag Duff, Model proposed the Third Amendment to the Eunion's Revised Criminal Code. E-Com was supposed to give its recommendation to Parliament before the Code was enforced throughout the EU on January 1st, 2020.

'It is the work of the Devil. This is a Holy Crusade.'

She couldn't quite scan Duroc. Sometimes, he seemed to assume comradeship with her as a fellow religious, though Modelists – especially ex-Catholics – were obliged to damn Pope Georgi as 'dangerously soft on hellfire'. Sometimes, she was sure Duroc put on an Ominous Warning act, subtly mocking those who expected 'thou ' and 'thine' of him.

'The Reverend has decreed we must put away Evil Things.'

Duroc was an ex-cop: after the Europa Defence Forces, he had been with Interpol, specialising in transnational serial murder. He had put away three of the Hackwill Killers: Pietro Moschone, Nadja Thiel, Hugh Best.

Duroc's law enforcement background, not his standing in the Modelist Church, earned him his place on E-Com. Jerome's company had informal ties with media consortia, which meant he balanced Duroc. As of now, the vote was split: Duroc for, Jerome against; like any Swiss, she was neutral.

Though resident in Vatican City, she did not hold an EU passport. Whatever E-Com recommended, the Amendment would not apply in her homeland.

'It's not like Virtual Reality,' she said. 'Except in the generic way television is like theatre.'

'The Industry cognits Mimesis is the Real Thing.' said Jerome, holding the dreamsphere. It was a pleasing bauble, a flawless silver pearl. 'VR was a side-track. All you could do was chuck things at customers' heads or let them wander around CGNvironments. Remember when "interactive" was the buzz? That was Big Mistake Uno. Punters want *stories*, not choices. Once they got past redoing *This is Cinerama!* and zotzing aliens, every-fool zoned out of VR. That's why it's taken two decs to develop Mimesis. When all those Millennium VR parlours went belly-up, research funding dried. If not for Derek Leech's deep pockets, we wouldn't have the tech. And if Mimesis rockets faster than zonk cocaine, it still won't show a profit before 2050. Then again, Leech can afford it.'

'This is like being someone else, Jerome. No, not like being. Like being in someone else's head.'

The stick figure of Tina Singleton came to mind.

'Same effect reading *Pamela* two-point-five centuries back, Sister Chan. Or auditing an Oedipus or Hamlet soliloquy. The diff is it isn't just words now. You're not on the outside, empathising. You're on the inside, sharing.'

'It's the work of the Devil,' said Duroc.

'Or Derek Leech, which Mum says is the same thing,' said Jerome. 'Then again, Leech's Cloud 9 Satellite Net carries Reverend Model's tele-ministry.'

Though there were no mirrors in the scene she had dreamed through, the viewpoint carried a self-image icon. Beneath the Hollywood cheerleader face, Chantal intuited a template with which she was familiar.

'Tina looks like Marthe Wink, don't you think?'

Marthe Wink was the Hamburg victim.

Jerome was startled. 'There are resemblances; then again, there are differences.'

Duroc said nothing.

Chantal found the file on the desk. She flipped it on and called up post-mortem glossies.

The phantom intrusion in her shoulder matched a wound in Marthe's shoulder. The gouge was a 3-D rose through the wrong side of a stereoscope, a hole ribbed with red folds.

'We mustn't be too dazzled by the tech or the aesthetic,' she said. 'Mimesis is just breaking. There's so much to cognit about how it works, what its potential might be. What we have to decide is whether it turns dreamers into murderers.'

After two years studying *Where the Bodies Are Buried* kill clusters, Chantal was still unsure of the Hackwill Effect.

In Vatican screenrooms, she re-familiarised herself with all thirteen films; meanwhile, tapping into archives, she immersed herself in seemingly every incidence of homicide that occurred during the fifteen-year run of the series.

The Hackwill Effect began as a newsnet scare patterned on long-running tabloid rumours that certain blues or heavy metal audio-tracks were conducive to suicide, but evidence accrued like coral. Some people who watched *Bodies* films went out and committed atrocities. Rob Hackwill reached out from screens to warp minds, making monsters of random members of the audience. Undeniably, there were murders. Equally undeniably, following a newsbite lead, it was claimed in court – by prosecution and defence – that murderers were under the influence of the bogeyman.

She scrolled through a mediamorass of interviews with 'Hackwill Killers'. The most interesting was the most talkative: Elizabeth Yatman gave a bookfile of detail about how Hackwill had turned her into a mass murderess. But Chantal intuited in Yatman's references an evasiveness that suggested only sketchy, second-hand knowledge of the films. No

Hackwill fanatic would confuse Tina Singleton with Stacey Snyder, but Beth Yatman did.

Yatman, nearly fifty, was thriving in England's Broadmoor Facility, happily claiming 'Hackwill made me do it' to Backchat Sites, making encouraging noises to the pressure group campaigning for her release. An accomplished cook, she sent cakes to supporters, and also to Relatives of Hackwill Victims spokesfolk. RHV hardly needed to campaign for her continued incarceration.

Chantal was inclined to class the Hackwill Effect a modern instance of Loudon or Salem Hysteria, an arbitrary shifting of guilt onto something beyond self. Instead of the Devil, a string of tame horror films were singled out and blamed for atrocities conceived and executed by apparently normal people. The oldest, saddest excuse of all: 'I was only obeying orders.'

Cardinal Kevin Menzies, her supervisor, allowed her thesis to be a first public acknowledgement that the Vatican had ever considered the Hackwill Effect. She seconded the findings of a *sub rosa* 2004 inquiry which recommended Yatman's request for exorcism be ignored. Not refused, *ignored*. The plea was one of Yatman's increasingly bizarre attempts to remain Site Prime News. Besides, Rob Hackwill was not officially recognised as a demon, nor was ever likely to be.

There was still *something* about the *Bodies* films. Something unhealthy, if not unholy.

Yatman, like two other Hackwill Killers – one of whom was never caught – murdered in and around the English backwater where Allan Keyes, writer-director of the original *Where the Bodies Are Buried*, had grown up. Lesley Conyers, victim of the unsolved Hackwill killing, was once Keyes's girlfriend. Another murderer was *called* Robert Hackwill. His name had lodged in Keyes's memory from childhood, resurfacing arbitrarily in his fiction.

Could it be something in the water?

Or maybe the popularity of the *Bodies* films was not causal to the Hackwill Killings but parallel with them. Both might be symptoms of something else.

It was not Hackwill that unnerved her: once she was past adolescence, he struck her as an obvious loser with a stale repertoire. More disturbing was the Devil Princess, Hackwill's infernal mistress. It said much about Keyes's psyche that he chose to depict Ultimate Evil as a provocative teenage fillette who wore black leather and chains or a scarlet nun's habit.

Maybe it was the mediaeval architecture around her as she worked, but at the root of the Hackwill Effect was something that made her yearn to leave the Post-Modern Papacy of Genial Georgi and take refuge in a Vatican which believed in physical war with the armies of the Devil.

While working on the thesis, she dreamed often.

Her conclusion, deleted from the final draft at Menzies's request, was that the church not rely on psychology in dealing with the resurgent Hackwill Effect, but fall back on ancient, spiritual resources.

Her now-cautious thesis was modestly posted on the Vatican branch of the World-Tree just as Morag Duff, on the point of yielding the EU chair to Czechskanzler Martina Drnkova, set down the Amendment as a parting gift to her successor.

'For century kiddettes like me, Information is Air, Chantal. We breathe it in from birth.'

Jerome had finally not called her Sister. For her, a little triumph.

'Actually, Mum's a Nouveau Luddite. Won't have a flatscreen in the apartment. Never downloads newsbits.'

'You're probably reacting to her.'

'She taught me not to surrender to white noise, to scan only for what matters. Then again, usually I intuit *when* gen matters but not *why*. That, I cognit, is your job description.'

They were at a pavement café in the Ghetto. An electric brazier melted the thin snow back metres away from their table, and created a bubble of warmth. A maché golem, creaking with every move, served tall glasses of hot tea. Jerome played with his Kafka Salad, picking out chocolate roaches.

The tottering Expressionist walls and tiny alleyways were processed styro, spray-coated to mimic ancient stone. Cabalist graffiti art covered every surface. The place was less than ten years old, an exact recreation of an original razed early in the last century.

All the capitals of Eunion were becoming theme parks; even the Vatican. Sub-national congresses passed laws requiring citizens to wear 'traditional' costume in public. Australasian tourists expected it.

Nearby, *Robotas* – in the original Czech sense, indentured workmen not machines – were restoring the frontage of a vandalised Synagogue Gift Shop by abrading deep-etched, luminous Anti-Semitic slogans. Throughout the Ghetto, there were rumours of a *pogrom* coming. Few Jews lived here, but misethnicists had as much contempt for the Mongols and Kurds collected in the beehive-cell apartments stacked above these streets.

A giant head popped into being above a public holo-plate. Waves of white hair around a withered angel face, eyes augmented by burning azure overlays.

'It's Roger's boss,' Jerome commented. 'The Model Man.'

Joseph Model was the most successful E-Vangelist. He synthesised saleable qualities perfected by US tele-ministries of the last century, but preached Old World Puritanism and a Work Ethic that verged on Slavery. Doctrinally, an economic Calvinist; politically, a Mussolini fascist; he liked to compare himself with Savonarola, Malcolm Muggeridge and Rush Limbaugh.

The holo began speaking, simultaneously in Hebrew and Czech, about the uprising in Cadiz. Model harshly criticised EU refusal to let his relief-workers deploy in combat zones. In a rare moment of passion, Pope Georgi had described Modelist Rapid Response Teams as 'spiritual looters'. During the Basque Insurrection, RR Teams dispensed medical help and subsistence food only in exchange for signatures on lifetime contracts with the Modelist Ministry.

'I can't scan Roger,' Jerome admitted. 'Why is he with Model? He seems too clued to be a Zombie.'

'I've heard that said about me.'

'Georgi's made it snazz to be a nun, Chan. His renunciation of the doctrine of Papal Infallibility is a major break with deadhead tradition. Then again, liberalism might erode core strengths.'

'Strictly speaking, I'm a priest, not a nun. That's another Georgi reform for you.'

'I'm sorry. It's hard sometimes to rewrite the program.'

'Worry not. Many in the church have the same problem.'

Model was talking about the Amendment now, another declaration of intent with case histories. She caught the name 'Marthe Wink'.

'Scans like Roger reported back.'

She agreed.

'Then again, I imagine the Modelists have access to as much gen as we do.'

It turned out Marthe was one of a group of tech-buff teens who had rigged up their own dreamdeck and got hold of bootleg dreamspheres from the States. The night before her murder, the girl had dreamed *Where the Bodies Are Buried*. Model made much of the similarities between Tina Singleton's encounter with Hackwill and the actual killing.

'He's distorting the story,' Jerome said. 'Tina's the viewpoint throughout. Hackwill doesn't kill her in the first scene, just marks her.'

Model announced that Marthe's parents were co-chairing the revived Relatives of Hackwill Victims Group and supporting the Model-Duff Amendment. The financial recompense to which they would be entitled if the Amendment became law was unimportant, the E-Vangelist said, because the Winks were independently wealthy. They just wanted those responsible for their daughter's death to be held culpable. Any settlement received from Pyramid Releasing – Model actually named the Leech Company – would be donated to the Ministry's Spiritual War Chest.

'So if his law gets passed, Model is in line for a credit injection. Then again, he's already independently wealthy too.'

In its fifteen years existence, Modelism had become the second richest church in the world. If his petition to assume temporal leadership of Liechtenstein was allowed, Model would be in a position to challenge Rome. Cardinal Menzies, only half joking, suggested the Vatican develop First Strike capability against the day the Modelist standard went up in Vaduz.

She found Eurocash in her purse and settled the addition. Swiss francs or Australasian dollars would be more welcome, but Eurocrats could not afford to betray the currency.

Model was harping on 'malign Asiatic influences'. One of the *robotas* heaved a bucketful of styrodust and grubby frozen snow into the Model head, disrupting the holo-link. Patches of see-through speckled the head like measles. The *robota* was a Mongol, one of the Genghis Khan trail refugees produced by the Sino-Tibetan crisis. His gesture was cheered by many bystanders, but a black-suited 'missionary' at the next table looked on grimly, noting faces.

The holo-head kicked into its pre-programmed appeal for all the Faithful to dedicate their worldly goods to Modelism, noting both the Biblical imprecation to 'store up treasures in Heaven' and Liechtenstein's liberal tax regime. At the same time, Model scorned the poor, the sick, the stricken. If God made some people victims, then that was His business and should not be argued with. In His wisdom, God had set up tollgates on the road to Heaven.

'I love God so much, Jerome,' she said, surprised at herself. 'Through my life, that has been my strongest relationship. It's never gone away. I've never doubted, not for a second...'

Model offered sacraments of wealth and immortality. A credit card hotline number flashed on his forehead.

'... so why do I find it so easy to hate religion?'

In the dream, Tina survived but the Mark of Hackwill was on her shoulder. She alone in Spring Meadow knew the monster's face. Chantal was almost used to riding viewpoint now; comfortable in the dreambody, lulled along.

Mind-chewing over her midnight encounter, Tina walked down the corridor towards the lockers. The set was dressed with posters for the Junior Prom. Kids passing by wore 2019 fashions – box suits and skunk-stripes – and toted set-books, but the dreamscene was classically archetypal. Tina – tartan skirt, white blouse, ankle socks – would pass as a teen queen in any of the last eight decs.

A hand fell on her aching shoulder. Chantal's heart leaped as Tina jumped. She whirled, prepared to face Hackwill, and was relieved to see her best friend, Stacey Snyder.

'What's word, humming bird?' Stacey chirruped.

'What's tale, nightingale?' Tina replied.

Arm-in-arm, the girls walked to their lockers, turning boyheads as they passed. Chantal's own secondary school in Geneva had been shaped by US mediamass into a multi-lingual imitation of Spring Meadow High. Some of the extras wore the faces that furnished her memories.

'You scan devastaté, Teen. Hard night with Jimmy T?'

'One hopes.'

Chantal looked side-on at Stacey. Like all the supporting characters, she was almost totally convincing. An actress would have leased herself as a template for CGIdentity, converting her likeness and the character tics of a specific performance into a stream of infobits. Now the dream, orchestrated by a computer-assisted Talent, was recycling information as a semi-autonomous illusion.

'Serious, girlchik. You scan like Death on Drugs.'

'I had ... bad dreams.'

'Condolences.'

'Processed and perfected.'

Chantal was fluent in French, Italian, English, German, Latin and Japanese; and had a working knowledge of a dozen other tongues. She found Hollywood teenspeak hard to follow.

Processed and perfected.

Tina's locker, where Hackwill notes had been delivered, loomed large in visionfield. A subliminal thrum of dread built up suspense as she approached.

Stacey blithely opened her locker and pulled out her set-book. She shook it, disrupting the fog-pattern on the screen, and tapped in the code for the biology text.

'Ugh,' she said. 'It's anelids.'

Tina looked at her locker. She tapped entrycode on the keypad and the lock clicked free.

'S'matter, Teen? You got Jimmy's severed head stashed?'

Tina took out her set-book. The message icon was blinking at her. She meant to stab DELETE, but knew she would spend the day wondering. She accessed the message and the cut-up letters appeared on the set-book's screen.

2-niTE's Sta-C's NIGHT.

'What's it process, Teen?'

Tina looked at Stacey. A superimposition skull flashed on her pretty-pretty face. In Tina's head, Hackwill's laugh sounded.

'Absolute Secret, huh?'

Tina hugged Stacey, hard.

'Care, Stace. Take chance none. For me, please.'

'Nichevo, Teen. It's only anelids. I can process and perfect.'

'No, not that. Really care.'

A frozen moment: Tina pulled back and looked again at Stacey's open face, fixing it poignantly in memory.

From the original film – where the notes were on paper not screen – if not this heavy foreshadowing, Chantal knew Stacey would be Hackwill's next victim.

She told herself Stacey was a simulacrum wearing the face of a woman now auditioning for better roles, but it was still a wrench: tonight, this girlchik would die.

TRANSITIONAL FADE

Even Mimesis could not make it scan as real. When Tina shut her eyes, she was in school in the morning, warmed by sunlight glimmering through windowwalls; when she opened them a subjective blink later, it was after dark and she was outside her house, wearing a heavy coat against the cold.

Like theatre and cinema, Mimesis cut and pasted bits of narrative into scenes unfolding faster than life. The irony was that it was technically easier to provide convincing, unedited actuality, but there wasn't a market. In realwelt, too much time is wasted getting from place to place, feeding and cleaning, doing nought. This was reality edited for length, doled out in suspenseful slices.

Here, the dremake was departing from the first *Where the Bodies Are Buried*. The old film cut from the locker scene to Stacey later that day, receiving her own suggestive note, taking a lengthy – gratuitous – shower before dolling up for a date. In a dark scary house, she was stalked by Hackwill and turned limb by limb into a mannequin. A classic image from the film was her living eyes, trapped in a smooth plastic face, tears trickling down unfeeling cheeks.

Mimesis required the story be perceived from a single viewpoint. No cutting away to other characters, no privileging the audience with information withheld from the heroine. Right now, it was a first person medium. Jerome reported the Industry was experimenting with allowing the dreamer to hop from viewpoint to viewpoint, even choosing whom to ride through the plot. That was a generation or two down the line.

As Tina trotted nervously through the night, constantly scanning behind her, Chantal realised the dream was taking the easiest possible alternative. Tina was going to sneak into the dark scary house – the Old Hackwill Place, naturally – and witness the monster's torment of her friend.

When she wondered how Tina knew where Stacey was being lured, there was an annoying misty patch in the mind construct. Chantal recognised a program flaw. Whenever the dreamer spotted a logic lapse, the viewpoint threw up a strategic memory blank.

The Old Hackwill Place loomed. Tina stopped to look up at it, giving a visionfield of the major locale. It was a tridvid synthesis of every haunted house in every horror movie: from the rusted gate hanging by one hinge to the single light in a gable window, the stone eagle over the doorway to the bricked-up room in its own turret.

Beyond the house was the graveyard where Hackwill had been caught and tortured by the mob. Chantal was getting ahead of the story; presumably, that flashback would come later, when Tina got suspicious enough to track down Judge Jonathan and get the story out of him.

Chantal's impatience made Tina walk fast forward. The front door opened by itself and she stepped inside the house. A scream abused her ears.

ERROR

The scream caused some kind of playback fault. Chantal lost Tina and found herself back in realwelt. The heavy hoodset was giving her a crick in the neck.

This time, she was alone. But she had the sense someone had been in the cabin with her and just stepped out.

More authentically spooked at that than by the cliché horror house, she considered getting up and looking into the walkway outside. It ran the length of the *Meyrink*. Her visitor – if visitor there had been – should still be in sight.

Could it be Jerome? Subotai?

The hoodset was too heavy. A design fault. She didn't want to get up. She twisted around, looking for the remote, and found it clipped to her breast pocket.

She tapped **RUN**.

Tina stood, fear-frozen, in the doorway. Before her was a tableau.

On the stairs Stacey writhed, dead legs dragging. On the landing, looking down, was Rob Hackwill.

Tina watched the transformation continue. Stacey's elbows kinked the wrong way and became notched-and-pinned joints. She held fingers to her face and gasped as they became bone-like chunks of wood, strung together on wires.

Stacey looked to her friend for help.

Tina was rigid. Chantal was irritated at the dream's assumption of girly uselessness. Tina made no move to help or comfort Stacey.

Stacey's face stiffened and drained of colour. It was the crying mannequin image, recreated in tridvid. Chantal realised the moment was somewhat thrown away.

Mimesis distanced her from Stacey, trapping her in Tina. In the original, there was a powerful sense of loss. Not least because the actress playing Stacey was better than the inept ex-model cast as Tina. As a viewer, Chantal knew with Stacey's death that her pleasure in the balance of the film would be limited by the lack of the character.

Now, Chantal was confused. She couldn't be frightened for Tina because she realised, even if the dremake diverged radically from Allan Keyes's old script, she was fundamentally safe. If the viewpoint died, the dream would end.

Suddenly, she realised she was invincible in the dreamwelt. With a surge of courage, she looked up at Hackwill, knowing him for a cardboard fiend. He had no power over her, in realwelt or this shoddy simile.

The monster stepped into the light. He moved like a human snake, hissing through lipless smile, red eye winking. Talons grooved scratches in the banister.

Hackwill prodded the Staceyquin with a toe-point. In a tangle of loose limbs and twisted clothes, the dummy rolled downstairs. Twisted around, the head looked up, eyes pools of anger, face cracked across. A beetle crawled out of the fissure, a gratuitously icky touch.

Tina stood her ground. Chantal wondered if she had short-circuited the dream by spotting the logic lapse. Would her realisation that the viewpoint could never be in mortal peril trigger a fast-forward to plot resolution?

'You think Robbie has no surprises left, don't you?' said the monster.

He stepped down to Tina and reached out. His claw-fingers lightly touched her face. His nailpoints were cold and sharp.

'We're to be great friends and collaborators, dearest. This rag doll is only the beginning. There'll be many others. And the work we have to do is such fun.'

Hackwill wasn't like Stacey. Up close, he had a different texture. There was something super-real about him, a fuzziness in the detail. He shifted through levels of reality, catching the light differently from moment to moment, like silk or falling rain. He was not like an actor in a close-fitting latex monster mask, any more than he was like a real disfigurement victim.

Hackwill leaned close to her and whistled softly through his bare teeth. She saw his red eye up close, and intuited something unique in its depth. She caught a whiff of gravemold under a strong cologne.

'We're partners, Sister...'

The sibilants of *ssissster* were razor kisses. Panic seized her.

Everything spun out of control.

'Come now,' Hackwill chided. 'Did you think I wouldn't recognise you, Chantal. We're old friends.'

STOP BREAK

'He calls her "Tina"', Jerome said. 'Well, he calls me "Tina" when I dream it. Then again, there are playback variants. It's to do with the interface between Mimesis and your back brain. It's always been metaphorically true; now it's literally so. Consciousness is inescapably subjective. We all see things differently: a tree, a painting, a girl.'

'Hackwill knew me,' Chantal insisted.

Jerome had dreamed through the scene carefully. He was genuinely concerned. He trusted her word. The monster had talked to her. Not to Tina, to her. Like a good information processor, Jerome was not denying the input but trying to interpret it.

In its blackwood and red velvet box, the dreamsphere was inert. Chantal's reflection distorted in its curved surface.

She was not quite ready to go back and dream the Dark Scary House scene again.

'Maybe it's a programming glitch. *Bodies* is pre-release. This is only a test impression.'

'I didn't feel alone in there.'

'You're intuiting the presence of the Talent. It's impossible to erase entirely.'

'Who is the Talent?'

'Ultimately, Allan Keyes. He's the dreamshaper. Augmented by tech-assists. Maybe he's just a marquee name, and subsidiary Talents do the actual shapework. Not everyone can be a Talent. It's inborn.'

Chantal knew about Allan Keyes. Rob Hackwill was his life's work. Obviously, he was still with the program.

'We'll have to take testimony from him.'

Jerome smiled. 'It's fixed. Pyramid are setting up a Virtual Pow-Wow. Us here, Keyes in La-La Land. Wonders of Modern Science.'

She got up and looked out of the porthole. A restaurant floated by, trailing balloons under the Charles Bridge. On each balloon was the face of the Dalai Lama over crossed Armalite-99 rifles. It was a fund-raiser for yet another Church Militant.

'Where's Duroc?' she asked.

'He left a holonote. His Interpol sources slipped him pre-release news and he's hared off to Barcelona. Dark hints, hush-hush. He says it's a relevant mission.'

'Relevant to us, or Model?'

'Mr and Mrs Wink, the Euro-Commission extends deep condolences for your loss.'

'Thank you, Sister,' said Herman Wink.

Chantal wished Duroc were here. Herman and Monika Wink, flanked by Modelist bodyguards, spoke mostly through a lawyer whose single-piece was fastened by tiny tags.

The couple did not strike Chantal as especially upset, but people took losses in their own way. Most of the other parents were unable to give testimony, spasming with uncontrolled grief or mind-blanked by sedation. The Winks were the official spokesfolk of Relatives of Hackwill Victims. Their Pro-Amendment petition was still downloading.

'We take comfort that Marthe was of the Last Generation,' Monika Wink said. 'Her transgression was justly rewarded, but her lapse will guide others.'

Jerome covered the audio and talked to Chantal, 'I'm not understanding this. Transgression? Lapse?'

As Modelists, the Winks believed their daughter marked herself for death simply by sampling the dream. By being murdered, she had cleansed herself and would be redeemed. Model always used the analogy of investment, referring to those judged favourably by the Lord as wise savers whose investment had matured. Those who sinned were spendthrifts whose earthly poverty would extend into the afterlife. Extreme suffering of the flesh could, in certain cases, wipe out the heaviest of debts.

'It is certain Marthe dreamed *Where the Bodies Are Buried*?'

Herman nodded. Chantal thought a flicker of genuine hurt crossed Monika's face.

'This is so,' Herman admitted. 'She was led into Evil Ways by unhealthy associations. The Reverend Model has proscribed Mimesis as a Tool of the Devil, but Marthe would not see the wisdom. She was wilful.'

Marthe's murderer was still unknown and at large. I-Pol established he was the same person known to be responsible for at least sixteen other killings, throughout the Eunion, within the last two years. The newsnets inevitably tagged him as a Hackwill Killer. The murders began at about the time Pyramid announced *Bodies* would be remade in Mimesis. Three of the last five victims had, like Marthe, contact with bootlegs.

'We comfort ourselves that our daughter's death serves a high purpose, Sister,' Herman Wink said. 'This Evil Thing will be destroyed.'

'We thank you,' said Jerome.

The Winks' lawyer broke the link. The holo-projections of the witnesses and their entourage vanished.

Chantal and Jerome sat alone in the hearing room. She loosened her collar.

'They were a piece of work,' Jerome said.

She flipped on Marthe Wink's file, scrolling through the forensics, calling up pre-death clips. She had looked like her mother.

'This isn't about them, Jerome. This is about Marthe. And the others.'

She was on deck, reading her breviary. After fourteen years, daily duty came easily. As a novice, she had scrubbed cell floors between masses and her secular studies. Though clerical celibacy was abolished, it was no wonder few priests married. Who had the time?

'Chan, excuse me...'

It was Jerome, with something important. He knew the breviary was her one inescapable daily commitment.

'Some Czechs have come aboard. They want to throw Subotai over the side.'

She had been aware, distantly, of the commotion.

'Modelists?'

'No, regular fascisti.'

'How many?'

'Three.'

They walked around the deck. The fascisti – teenagers with Rommel coats, swastika-tat scalps and top hats – had Subotai up against the rail. The E-Com cook and one of the secretaries – both Czechs who openly despised the Mongol – were watching, not making a move.

She tried to conquer her anger.

Obviously, the fascist not holding Subotai, prepared to let her comrades do the tossing-overboard for her entertainment, was leaderine. She was a heavy-set girlchik with steroid biceps and blonde Viking plaits.

Without saying anything, Chantal walked into the situation and angled a high kick at the underside of leaderine's chin, sticking the point of her pump into softness.

The fascist staggered, dizzy, gulping. Jerome was equally astonished. The girlchik growled – she had a jewel skull inset in an incisor – and Chantal ducked under an attempted wrestling-grasp. She heaved up, thumping Valkyrie sternum with her shoulder.

The leaderine went over the side with a satisfying splash, crashing through a thin ice-lily.

'As Devil Princesses go, not very impressive, *hein*?'

Chantal chided herself for enjoying the moment.

The other two let Subotai go.

'My vows oblige me to forgive you your sins, but not forget them. You may leave by the gangway and fish out your wet friend. Good day.'

The kids bolted. Subotai nodded impassive thanks and returned to whatever he had been doing.

'We were lucky,' she told Jerome. 'Modelists wouldn't have been seen off so easily. Religion gives a lot of idiots strength.'

Jerome was admiring her.

'Chan, I can't decide whether you remind me more of Audrey Hepburn in *The Nun's Story* or Diana Rigg in *The Avengers*? I'm sorry. Those references don't mean anything to you, do they?'

She laughed. He always forgot her field was pop culture.

'In Switzerland, *The Avengers* is called *Bowler Hat and Kinky Boots*. It was on all the time when I was little. And every woman with the calling has to see *The Nun's Story* when they're nine. I saw it back-to-back with *The Red Shoes* and was torn between becoming a saint or a prima ballerina.'

Duroc's head sat on the plate. Chantal and Jerome held still, so their faces were caught in the link-beams. Agitated talkers lost ears and noses over holo.

'The Hackwill Killer is in the city,' Duroc said.

'We're conferencing with Keyes tomorrow,' Jerome said. 'Can you tap in from Barcelona?'

'It is not likely,' Duroc replied. 'Thy report will be accepted.'

His face was blank. He accepted holo but Virtual Conference was too close to Mimesis. She wondered if he was tempted to sample a dream. She and Jerome dipped in and out of *Where the Bodies Are Buried* all the time, but Duroc was required by contract with the tele-ministry to abjure Mimesis. The Modelist must at least be curious. He was still human.

The head vanished.

'His cop genes are taking over,' Jerome said. 'These cases were his specialty.'

With his background, I-Pol Barcelona must be glad to have Duroc. From his involvement with the Moschone, Thiel and Best cases, he was up to speed on Hackwill Killers.

'He knows about us,' she said.

'Duroc?'

'The killer. He's following E-Com. The first murder was just after the Model-Duff Amendment was proposed. Jeanine Csathó, the Budapest victim. All the killings have been inside the Eunion. If Model-Duff becomes law, it will only be enforced within the EU.'

'Gets bigger every year. If Libya is admitted, it'll open up the rest of North Africa. The only hold-out is your place.'

'There are no Swiss victims. He's killed from Gibraltar to Greenland, from Ankora to Yeltsingrad. Why not Zurich, or Tel Aviv, or Cuba? The *day* after Bermuda came in, he killed there. It's as if he's drawing a map.'

'He doesn't want to go through passport control.'

'He'd have needed a passport to get to Bermuda before killing McCharen.'

'You're beginning to sound like a Hackwill Killer yourself. Do you really think Rob Hackwill is talking to you?'

'This is realwelt, Jerome.'

'I'm sorry, Chan. I'll have to process this. You have to admit it scans paranoid at first scroll-through.'

'You, me and Duroc. We're between two huge grinding cliffs of credit. On the one side, a hugely wealthy Industry: the Derek Leech Group is richer than most countries. On the other, the Relatives of Hackwill Victims, underwritten by the Modelist tele-ministry. These killings have been going on since the last century. If Model-Duff gets on the statutes in the EU, RHV will bring multiple suits. If cases go their way, there'll be a credit transfer bigger than the one that caused the Nikkei Crash of 2014.'

'I know all this, Chan. We have to focus on micro-issues. The Amendment. We recommend or not on its own merits. Think of the victims. Think of the victims who are still alive, who haven't been born yet.'

The idea wasn't original to Joseph Model and Morag Duff: it had been proposed in America as early as the 1990s. It was to do with blame and compensation: if murderers were shaped not born, then the forces which influence them should share culpability. If a rapist's mind was warped by pornography, then a rape victim should be able to sue pornographers. The Model-Duff Amendment proposed moral guilt be brought under a legal remit.

It was a simple, appealing idea. Yet it frightened her.

The Barcelona Victim was called Armando De Castro Oros. Duroc downloaded stats before the newsnets got them.

Hours before the scheduled Virtual Conference, Chantal was praying for guidance. No matter how she tried to clear her mind, De Castro Oros remained.

The boy was found dressed as a schoolgirl, face coated with asphyxiating plastic. Post mortem, his murderer had cracked the fast-setting mask and jammed in a chocolate beetle. The victim's tears were trapped bubbles in the plastic.

He was a Stacey. Like Victor McCharen, Saira Matsoela and Laure Petietich.

The killer was repeating victim types: Tinas, Staceys, Jimmy Traynors, Judge Jonathans, Boss Hoopers. All the characters from the dream.

There was no other connection between De Castro Oros and *Where the Bodies Are Buried*. If there was a black market dreamsphere in Barcelona, I-Pol had not found it.

Duroc was returning to Prague by way of Bermuda, where he wanted to follow up on McCharen. An American tourist, the Bermuda Victim might have been a smuggler, responsible for getting the dreamspheres into the EU in the first place.

For Chantal, prayer was a communion. Like Jerome processing random infobits, she could sometimes run through the elements of a problem and be led to a conclusion in something approaching a vision.

Not today.

Chantal would have been satisfied with a holo-link, swapping tridvid with Beverly Hills. Pyramid, wanting to impress E-Com with tech, insisted on a fancier Virtual Conference.

They were to meet Allan Keyes in Spring Meadow. Jerome, excited, explained the *Bodies* dreawmwelt could be accessed as a non-narrative CGNvironment. It was a supplementary feature of Home Mimesis dreamspheres, along with a bound copy of the script and collector's cards.

Jerome sat on the couch, adjusting his hoodset. He had already helped her plumb in.

'You won't be a *dybbuk* this time, Chan. You'll have autonomy.'

'But I'll still be Tina.'

Jerome nodded, hoodset bulbous. 'Since *Bodies* is a single viewpoint dream, so will I.'

Her eyepieces descended, blanking her vision. A test signal blipped into her brain.

'Ready?' Jerome asked.

She was back in the park, standing before the statue, waiting for midnight. As she slipped into the Tina simile, Chantal prepared for a mindlink that did not come. For a moment, she thought the puppet's strings were cut and she would fall in a tangle. Then, she was in control.

She was herself, but with Tina's dreambody.

By the statue stood a pretty girl in a heavy coat and a wool scarf. She smiled and shrugged.

'Weird,' Jerome commented, through the pretty girl's mouth. 'This

gets stranger.'

Jerome-as-Tina looked a little different from the self-image of Chantal-as-Tina. She saw Jerome's slenderness in his simile, even an underlay of his cheekbones in the Tina face.

She wondered if Allan Keyes and the Pyramid CEO would also be forced to be Tinas. Probably not; at their end, they would have more sophisticated dreamtech and should be able to select viewpoints to suit themselves.

She looked around, dreamflesh creeping.

'What's up, Chan?'

'There's someone here.'

'They're not online yet.'

'No, not them.'

He glanced about too, and shrugged again. His distinctive smile stretched the Tina face.

'It's the first scene feeling, from the dream,' she explained. 'When Hackwill is creeping up on Tina.'

'The story isn't in RUN. For once, there's no Robbie here.'

'"There's always a Hackwill in Spring Meadow."'

'A-ha. Judge Jonathan's speech. You're a *Bodies* buff. I keep forgetting.'

Beeptone came from their coats. Jerome found his set-book before Chantal found hers. Both lit up with identical messages.

ThE olD HaCKwill playCE.

'Do you want to walk, or...?'

'Skip that,' she said. They both blinked...

TRANSITIONAL FADE

... and were outside the Dark Scary House. Stacey, a walking mannequin, was waiting for them on the porch. She had blots of rouge on white plastic cheeks.

'Mr Rhodes, Ms Juillerat,' she said through stiff, barely-parted lips. 'I'm Medea Calm, of Pyramid Releasing. We're proud to have you in Spring Meadow.'

The similes shook hands. Medea's fingers were hard and unmoving.

'Sorry about this. I had hoped to rep myself as the Stacey of her cute scenes, not the Staceyquin. I actually look a little like the babe version. But we had a simile transfer glitch. The bugs will be worked out prontissimo. It's cutting edge tech.'

Chantal had expected a Pyramid exec to be more like the Devil Princess.

'Allan is inside, waiting.'

Medea hobbled lop-sided into the mansion. Jerome hung back a little to let Chantal in first. The hallway was as it was in the finale, hellfire burn-marks on the wall.

Someone stood in the dark at the top of the stairs.

'Allan,' said Medea-as-Staceyquin, 'Mr Rhodes and Ms Juillerat are from the Euro-Commission on the Model-Duff Amendment.'

'I've scrolled your thesis, Sister,' said Keyes. 'You make some points.'

He stepped forward into the light.

Chantal had expected Keyes to be Hackwill, but the Talent was in the simile of Japheth Jonathan, the corrupt judge who explains Hackwill's origins. Thankfully, he was not as last seen in the dream – head exploded by his own tongue swollen to the size of a watermelon – but as in his intro scene. Keyes must be about Jonathan's age, but newssims did not suggest other resemblance. The Judge was an impressively-eyebrowed character actor; Keyes was one of those nondescript Englishmen, Jerome grown not old but faint.

One of the Hackwill Victims was Keyes's own girlfriend: it must take something to continue weaving nightmares after that. Originally a novelist, Keyes had turned himself into a motion picture director and then a Mimesis Talent, extending the reign of Hackwill into fresh media.

'How does a Jesuit get to know so much about horror films?' he asked.

'My field of study is Media Influence. Genre horror is central to the discipline. The pioneer work of Martin Barker and Julian Petley in the 1990s...'

'But do you *like* horror? Do you like what *I* do?'

She tried to give an honest answer. 'While working on my thesis, I became so familiar with the material that I lost perspective on aesthetic or entertainment quality. But I first decided to be a Jesuit because of *The Exorcist*. As a child, I saw the original *Where the Bodies Are Buried*

– it was made the year I was born – on Cloud 9 TV. It gave me nightmares for weeks, but I pleaded with my parents to let me watch it again.'

'Your thesis could do with input from the little girl you once were. I intuit you regret a weakness for the films. Because of the Hackwill Effect.'

'Pyramid Releasing does not acknowledge the existence of the so-called Hackwill Effect,' Medea cut in. 'Many studies – including your own, Sister Juillerat – question a hypotheticised causal relationship between fictional and realwelt violence.'

'Our guests aren't interested in blipquotes, Medea,' Keyes said. 'Credit them with that.'

Medea continued, 'if you lump together so-called Hackwill Killings over the last twenty-five years, including those later established as unconnected, you have at most 400 murders. Five times that many died in the Reverend Model's Warsaw *pogrom* last year. And what about British Druids mustard-gassed by Special Branch in the solstice of '17? Joseph Model and Morag Duff should look to their own consciences.'

The lecture was pointed, but sounded strange from a life-sized broken doll.

'You've obviously given the Hackwill Effect thought,' Chantal said to Keyes. 'Yet you've continued with *Bodies*. It can't just be for the credit. Why do you do it? Why do you create only horrors?'

Keyes smiled sadly. 'What makes you think I have a choice?'

All around, hellfire exploded.

INTERFERENCE

The similes could be hurt. These flames bit harder than the pain analogues usual in dreams. Consciousness unfiltered through viewpoint, she was immersed in intense heat, blinding light, choking stench, nipping agony.

Jerome was patting out the flames on her arm. Medea had vanished, presumably breaking the link. Half of Jerome's Tina hair was singed off.

A burning beam fell between them and Keyes. He stood still in the inferno. She wondered if his simile was an empty freeze-frame. But his eyes moved.

The laughter of the Devil Princess poured out of the air, setting fires wherever it was heard. In the original, only the mansion was destroyed; in the dremake, most of Spring Meadow was consumed.

Windows burst outwards. Draughts of cold air whipped flames into spirals that entwined the two Tinas. Chantal and Jerome hugged, as if the heroine wanted to reunite her divided self.

'Another glitch?' Jerome asked.

In the fire behind Keyes, a black shape coalesced, rearing up over him, arms enfolding the Talent. Bands of clawed shadow held him fast. A single red eye shone, a crystal of fire in a man-shaped patch of night.

'Keyes!' she shouted.

Jerome thumped his own forehead, where the hoodset panel was in realwelt. He disappeared.

She was alone in Spring Meadow with Keyes and the Hackwill Effect. Fire rushed to fill the space where Jerome's Tina had been.

Allan Keyes – she could swear – smiled with almost relief as the shadow and flame wrapped around him. This was the end of his private dreamstory.

STOP

Jerome was pulling the hoodset off her. Half his face was an angry red.

She looked at her hands and saw white spots where cinders had scalded her in Spring Meadow.

Subotai was checking the fixed-up link, genuinely concerned for his temporary masters.

She intuited she had just experienced the downside of cutting edge tech.

'Do we still have audio-link?' she asked Subotai.

The *robota* stood aside and gave her the handset.

Jerome was swearing profusely in English, touching his pain patches. He was burned under unsinged clothes.

'Hello,' she said to the handset. 'Ms Calm? Keyes?'

There was a commotion at the other end.

'Ms Juillerat,' came a voice. A woman, shaky.

'Medea?'

'Uh, yes. We have no rationale for that ... uh ... incident.'

'Is Keyes out of the dream?'

'We've cut him off. He's here ... his body's here ... but there's nobody home.'

It was Site Prime in the weeks leading up to Halloween: Allan Keyes, the Hackwill Man, was the latest victim of the Hackwill Effect. His body might live but he was mindwiped, a human blank. Medicos theorised that if he came out of coma, he might develop from mental infancy, growing a new personality. But it was a moot point: he had suffered 78% burns in the Virtual Conference; if he came round, he would probably die from pain-trauma.

From the deck, Chantal looked down on grey waters. A drift of ground-hugging riot gas seeped down from the bridge, floating on the surface of the Vltava. She felt after-sting in her nostrils, even through the domino mask she wore when the pollution count was high.

Where the Bodies Are Buried had been recalled – E-Com had to surrender their dreamsphere to a notarised messenger – and Mimesis was on hold 'until bugs can be ironed out'. Whatever the truth of the Hackwill Effect, Keyes was proof that Mimesis could be hazardous to dreamers' health, mental and otherwise.

E-Com's ground was out from under them. The original inexpressed purpose of the enquiry, beyond even the Amendment, was to determine whether Mimesis be allowed unrestricted into Eunion. Now, Mimesis was withdrawn by the Industry: if Model-Duff passed, it would apply only to old-fashioned mediatech like motion pictures, tele and VR. Not newsworthy, but still a major legislative shift.

Using the railing as a *barre*, Chantal ran through ballet moves, stretching her legs until they felt real, making points of her toes. With the Troubles, she was advised not to go jogging up to the Castle and back as she had in E-Com's early days in the city. The *Meyrink* sometimes felt like a prison. She needed to maintain strength and suppleness. Exercise was a courtesy to God: it was her duty to maintain in peak condition the wonderful gift of a body her soul had been given.

As she felt the knots popping in her muscles and joints, she thought it over.

Duroc, back from his travels, was meticulously assembling an infodump about the current Hackwill Killings. He had taken their report of the Conference on board but had no ideas about it. To him, Mimesis dreams were hell equivalents even without brimstone.

Jerome thought it a glitch – bleedthrough from the narrative of *Bodies* – but Chantal was convinced there had been another presence in Spring Meadow. It was hard not to think of it as Rob Hackwill.

On the Charles Bridge, the demonstration turned ugly. Students, supporting persecuted refugees, clashed with Modelists, and armed police were caught between them. People fell or were tossed off the bridge, splashing in gas-covered water. Throwing malcontents into the river was a traditional Prague response to trouble; just as throwing bureaucrats out of windows was a traditional Prague way of making trouble. Last night, the head of the local Modelist Congregation had been defenestrated.

She stopped her program of kicks, and towelled her sweaty forehead. Through the domino, she breathed deeply.

The McDonald's Airport was shut down, transnational holo-links were out. After the Ghetto riots, Modelist Advance Teams combed the ruins, offering salvation with share options and low monthly payments. Subotai had heard a whisper that E-Com would have to share the *Meyrink* with an Europa Defence Force response unit straight from Cadiz.

Jerome came up on deck, looking sheepish. Turfed out of his hotel by a newsnet anchor, he was mooching around the ship, face glistening from the healing gel he had to wear until his burns faded.

'Chan, I've made my decision.'

She had expected this. The Spring Meadow Incident had shaken him. And the December deadline was approaching. She pulled off her domino so she could speak with him.

'I'm voting the Amendment be attached to the Revised Criminal Code,' he said. 'That aligns me with Roger.'

'I see.'

It didn't have to be unanimous. She still felt the enquiry should be pursued: Mimesis might even prove a side-issue to the greater question.

'As of now, I can't change my position,' she said.

'Still Swiss?'

She took the railing and kicked in the air, above Jerome's head. She had always had trick hips.

'I abstain. You know why.'

'I'm sorry, Chan.'

She went belowdecks to tell Duroc. At her knock, he unlocked his door.

Aside from the bunk, his cabin was furnished only with a flatscreen and a knee-rest. An official holo-bust of Reverend Model hovered under the bare lightstrip. Duroc worked always under the blind gaze of his master.

He stood aside to let her in. They both had to bow slightly because of the low ceiling. Duroc blithely dipped his head through Model, but Chantal avoided the holo as if it were a solid.

Duroc, alarmingly, was stripped to the waist. His back was striped with scars, some fresh. He had a scourge in his hand, a wicked cluster of studded flails with a riding crop grip.

She had not realised Duroc was a flagellant.

On the flatscreen were images Chantal recognised. A field laid out neatly with corpses. Black-clad Modelists prowling among the dead.

'The Basque Insurrection?' she asked.

Duroc nodded.

Most who had served in the Insurrection were soured on Modelists for life. There was a famous incident in which a non-com was court-martialled for disobeying orders and intervening to cut short a massacre supervised by elders of the tele-ministry.

Duroc must be Model's only convert from the EDF. No wonder he felt the need to whip himself.

'Jerome's changed his vote. To Yes.'

Duroc nodded, understanding.

'I'll prep a formal statement for Brussels. We all put our signatures to it. Then, we can go home.'

'Hast thou changed thy vote?'

'It doesn't have to be unanimous.'

'I know.'

He looked at her. She saw something hanging back in his eyes, but could not process it.

'Yes,' she admitted, 'I have changed my vote. From Abstention to No.'

She did not ask if Duroc wished to change his Yes to Abstention or No. That would have been futile.

'I'm sorry, Sister. We must all act in accordance with our conscience.'

He looked sideways at the Model head, as if seeking higher approval.

The decision was communicated on a priority line to Brussels, and the Model-Duff Amendment was attached to the Revised Criminal Code.

On New Year's Eve, Joseph Model held a celebratory rally in Vaduz. In his speech, he personally commended Chantal Juillerat, Jerome Rhodes and Brother Roger Duroc as Good Credit Christians. He claimed their Heavenly Portfolios were maturing exceptionally well, throwing off high-yield interests. He also promised arms to the Advance Teams in Prague, and accused Tel Aviv of inciting ghetto-dwellers to murder their Modelist rescuers.

The E-Com, officially dissolved, was still in Prague. Travel restrictions were in force until the fighting died down. On New Year's Day, there was a Hackwill Killing outside the Castle. Pavel Zahradnik, a Boss Hooper, head burned to the skull. His wife signed up with RHV. The Model-Duff Amendment – no, the Model-Duff Law – was retroactive: Petra Zahradnikova would have to join a queue of grieving, suing relatives.

The conglomerated lawsuit was already issued, and Pyramid's corporate attorneys were resisting attempts to bring the case to the European Court in Kiev.

Morag Duff, under fire for imposing an extension of the term between general elections to ten years, gloried in the success of her Amendment – she carefully never mentioned Model in public – and announced she would now devote herself to removing nudity from art galleries and British World Tree Sites. With lewdness and license expunged, she claimed – repeating her last electoral slogan – 'everything will be nice again'.

Chantal kept her cabin when the EDF unit moved in, but Duroc and Jerome had to bunk together. Subotai was pounced upon in the Square and severely beaten by Modelists. He was then removed to a camp in the Carpathians, where Czechskanzler Drnkova claimed refugees could be protected from violent mobs. Duroc did not to take part in any of his church's activities in the city, and shutters came down whenever the soldiers talked about the militia missionaries against whom they expected to be deployed.

Cardinal Menzies communicated that she was expected back in Rome when restrictions were lifted. She passed time with her breviary, unable to shift her mind from the dead issue of E-Com to her next task, finishing her Information Children bookfile.

She still sensed, just out of sight, the creature of flame and darkness that had attacked Allan Keyes in Spring Meadow.

'What are you scanning?' Jerome asked.

On deck, the EDF were doing push-ups. Duroc, twenty years older than most of the soldier kids, was earning respect by matching them thrust for thrust.

Jerome was frustrated; he missed spending the holidays with his mother. It seemed he would not get out of Czechia before Spring. Also, he was off-salary.

'I'm going through our logs, checking the hours we've put in at terminals and in meetings.'

'You think we've been rooked on our expenses?'

'Something nags.'

'Close it down, Chan. It's processed and perfected. We did our bit. Now it's up to lawyers.'

On St Valentine's Day, Subotai escaped from the Relocation Centre and made his way to Prague where, according to the newsnets, he was waylaid by the Hackwill Killer. He was a Judge Jonathan, head burst by a pressure capsule – intended for instant liferaft inflation – forced into his mouth.

Chantal was shocked and depressed. She liked and trusted the *robota*. Subotai's scattered family – and several women who repped themselves as his wives, but whose claims were instantly disproved – joined the RHV and added their lawsuits to the others. She intuited the case would not come to Kiev until the Hackwill Killer were caught.

Allan Keyes's condition remained stable.

On the *Meyrink*, it was hard to concentrate. She kept going over the logs of the E-Com. Jerome, suffering cabin fever, had taken to complaining about foreigners. The EDF – mostly Turks and Swedes – were growing nervy as their deployment was put off. Everyone was getting irritable.

Except Duroc. He exercised, read Modelist screentexts, and showed no interest in the world outside his faith.

It was Jerome who pointed out the anomaly.

'It's odd. Roger traipsed from Spain to Bermuda on the trail of the Hackwill Killer, but hasn't crossed the river to join the hunt now the murderer is in Prague. I'm surprised I-Pol haven't conscripted him to head the investigation.'

Just around midnight on March 1st, the alarum sounded. One moment, Chantal was in the *Meyrink*'s mess hall, improving her Swedish by chatting with a non-com from Malmo; then, she was surrounded by *Mary Celeste* detritus of abandoned card games and unfinished mugs of recaff.

The clattering of boots was a brief thunder. The ship actually rocked as the EDF unit assembled on one side of the deck. They yomped out, weighed down by weaponry, towards the Ghetto. She prayed for their safety. And for those they would be fighting.

Through the mess windows, she saw a glow in the sky. She had a flash of the Old Hackwill Place.

'They're burning the Ghetto,' Jerome said. 'The bloody fools. Modelist maniacs.'

Duroc was with them, showing no emotion.

Jerome turned on the Modelist. 'How can you be with those bloodthirsty credit-grubbers?'

'The Reverend Model tells us we must terminate unrewarding investments. Only radical measures will serve.'

'You can't really believe that scut!'

Duroc went up on deck.

In prayer, it came to her. The discrepancy that had been nagging was Duroc's trip to Barcelona.

She had to check first.

'Where are you going, Chan?'

She left Jerome in the mess hall and made her way down a deck.

The office was sealed but she still had a viable entry-code. She called up the logs on the terminal and scrolled them side-by-side with a newsnet chronology of the killings.

Jerome was in the doorway, puzzled. She was glad he had followed her. The ship lurched. A noise hammered: an explosion ashore, nearby. There was the popping of gunfire.

She concentrated on the screen, shutting out the macro-issues.

'Chan, what is it?'

'Look. Duroc arrived in Barcelona *before* Armando De Castro Oros was murdered.'

'He had an I-Pol tip-off?'

'No, he's the Hackwill Killer.'

There was a thump.

She turned from the screen and looked at Jerome's face. He was open-mouthed and wide-eyed, stunned. A trickle of blood came from his hairline. He stood statue-still, then pitched forwards.

Duroc, spanner in hand, stepped over Jerome and looked at her.

'I'm not a Hackwill Killer,' he said. 'There are no Hackwill Killers.'

As a teenager, ballet had lead for a while to martial arts. She saw the point in the centre of Duroc's solid chest where she should kick.

She stood slowly, tense but trying to calm herself. She knew she had no chance. Besides his training as a soldier, a policeman and a fanatic, Duroc was a practiced murderer. She could not hope to fight him.

'I'm doing the Lord's work,' he said, deadpan. 'As revealed to me by the Reverend Model. We must put away Evil Things.'

Was he mocking her?

He held the spanner loosely, thwacking his open palm with the heavy instrument.

Would she be a Tina or a Stacey?

He was a barrier in the doorway. That left her with one other option.

She made her move, grabbing the terminal chair and rolling it across the deck towards Duroc. It slammed him, not hurting at all, but distracting.

Chantal jumped and grasped with both hands a pipe that ran across the ceiling. She swung back and forth twice like an aerialist, feeling the *wrench* in her shoulders, then aimed herself feet-first at the porthole.

She was – thank God – wearing sensible shoes and a single-piece. Her points punched the circle of glass out of the hole and she followed through, body like a dart, praying hips or shoulders would not catch.

Fire raked her back as she plunged through the porthole, scraping herself on the rim. Her whole body was out in cold night when her wrists were grabbed.

Her shoulders exploded. Angry ants ate at the muscles from inside. For an instant, she thought her arms had come off.

Duroc held her, but her whole weight dragged her down. She slammed against the *Meyrink*'s steel hull. Bursts of shadow and flame obscured her visionfield.

This time, she was not a viewpoint. This was realwelt, with real pain and real death.

Her weight and momentum hauled Duroc partially out of the porthole. She looked up at his face and saw only shadow. The sky above the ship was crimson-streaked.

Somewhere else, guns were going off.

Duroc held her by the wrists, but couldn't haul her up without adjusting his grip.

'You never dreamed *Where the Bodies Are Buried*,' she said, through pain. 'You told me you never even saw the old film.'

'That is true.'

'Was it the Hackwill Killers you caught? You've been recreating their crimes?'

'There are no Hackwill Killers.'

It hit her that Pietro Moschone, Nadja Thiel and Hugh Best were innocent. Roger Duroc had framed them for earlier murder clusters.

'Roger, why?'

A fireburst illuminated the side of the ship, casting their harsh shadows on the hull. In red light, she glimpsed an upside-down smile playing around Duroc's lips.

'Sister, the Lord showed me the Way. Through Joseph Model.'

He dropped her.

She plunged into the filthy Vltava and felt she touched bottom before air in her lungs buoyed her. She struggled up through thick, freezing water. The ripples above were blobbed with reflected firebursts.

When she broke the surface, her ears were roaring. She swum to the bank, found an iron ring inset in a concrete wall, and pulled herself up, sopping, onto a jetty. Her single-piece stuck to her like a layer of clogged ice.

She wanted to curl up and get warm.

But she had left Jerome with Duroc.

She found the gangplank and ran up it, leaving dripping footsteps.

'Duroc!,' she shouted.

A bullet spanged against the hull of the *Meyrink*. A power-boat passed by, raising a white froth of wake. Someone fired another wild shot, not at her but at the sky.

'Praise the Lord and shoot the sinners,' shouted the boatman.

She had no idea what that was about.

She looked around for a weapon as she made her way down to the office deck. All she could find was a solid-body guitar. One of the Turkish soldiers had left it behind.

The corridor was quiet. She saw Jerome's legs, stuck out of the doorway. They shifted, as he was turned over.

Heart clenched, she ran to the office.

Duroc squatted by Jerome, examining his head wound.

'He'll be all right, Sister.'

She held the guitar by the neck, hefting it like a bludgeon.

'I've called the police. They're busy.'

With all her strength, she smashed the guitar into Duroc, lifting him off the floor.

As Duroc fell backwards, Chantal stepped through the door The lights went out and a chill fell on her. She blinked and held on to the neck of the broken guitar.

She was not in the office, with its burst porthole and dreamdeck, but back in the park in Spring Meadow. Duroc was sprawled at the base of the statue of the town founder.

He was not Duroc, but Hackwill.

Yet she was not Tina, but Chantal.

She stood over the monster, wondering whether to end it by driving the guitar neck through his heart. You could not kill Hackwill; he always came back for the sequel.

For some reason, the Modelist had been committing murders for years. Initially, he had used his position in I-Pol to frame others, tagging them as Hackwill Killers. It couldn't be the Hackwill Effect, unless it were a new strain, a Hackwill Effect By Proxy.

The monster was hurt, trying to lift himself.

'I said we had work to do, sissster,' he said.

She held the guitar-neck out like a crucifix to ward off Evil. Duroc supported himself by clinging to the pedestal. Bloody spittle hung from his mouth.

She guessed Duroc had intervened in the Virtual Conference, projecting into the dreamwelt through the thing of shadow and fire.

He was playing some immense game-plan.

And she had a horrid intuition that mass murder and E-Com and Model-Duff were merely facets of an intricate device whose purpose was not yet apparent.

Darkness and fire were contained in Duroc's thick chest, entwining his body with ropes of wavering black and red. He wore a transparent Hackwill mask. Behind it, his face was set.

She tossed the guitar-neck away and braced herself to fight.

In this waking dream, she was herself. She was still wet and hurt.

Pirouetting, she slammed her foot into his chest, imagining it a blunt knife, focusing her all into the kick.

Duroc coughed and thumped back against the statue.

Her ankle was badly jarred, but she ignored pain. Making triangular wedges of her fingers, she jabbed Duroc's torso where she had kicked, probing for broken spots.

Despite her blows, he stood up.

'I do the Lord's work,' he repeated.

He was completely shrouded in flame and shadow. Heat seared and cold stung her hands as she hit him. His Hackwill mask was illuminated from within, as if his skull were red hot beneath translucent flesh.

'May the Lord forgive you,' she said.

She punched him in the face and danced back away from him, knowing she couldn't keep this up much longer.

At the edges of the park, the dead gathered. The dead of *Where the Bodies Were Buried*: Stacey, Jimmy, the Judge, even Tina. And the dead of realwelt: Jeanine Csathó, Subotai, Marthe, McCharen, Zahradnik, De Castro Oros. Mannequinlike, the broken witnesses hobbled together.

Duroc stood still, relaxing, head hung slightly. She felt her anger fading.

Horror movie dead closed in, a shambling noose tightening around Chantal and Duroc. Allan Keyes was there, a ghost in his own dreamwelt, drifting above the grass. And the Devil Princess, hair like white flame spilling from her scarlet wimple.

The dream was running down.

'Where are we?' she asked.

'Outside, Sister,' the Devil Princess purred. 'In Spring Meadow, where the bodies are buried.'

Duroc spread his arms in surrender. Feathers of flame ran along their undersides. Fire and darkness gathered in Duroc's torso and coursed through his arms, exploding from his fingers, channelling into the dead, dissipating in the dream.

Duroc, empty, sagged at the knees, slumped at the feet of the statue. His face was pathetic, a childish plastic mask, broken across. His claws had come off too.

Rob Hackwill was only Roger Duroc dressed up.

Chantal stood over the murderer, feeling the tug of the realwelt beginning.

She knew now there was no Rob Hackwill. Just a man who had killed in the monster's name.

Suddenly, a laugh fell upon her from above, a laugh like a rain of hot pebbles. She knew instantly the cackle of the Real Rob. The pure evil of the old movies thrived. Hackwill still lurked in dreamspheres, scratching inside silver eggshell, to be born into the realwelt.

She looked up from the fallen Duroc to the greened bronze boots of the town founder. The statue creaked to life. A clawed hand raised a sword.

The burning red eye, the gnashing bloody teeth, the pouring laughter. Raised on his pedestal, Rob Hackwill ruled Spring Meadow.

Chantal fell to her knees and locked her hands in prayer.

She was back on the *Meyrink*, kneeling by the fallen Duroc, praying fiercely.

She must work swiftly.

As she tied Duroc up with cables from the dreamdeck, she worried at it in her mind. If it had been a vision, she intuited Duroc had shared it. Some of the dream had stuck in her mind and enveloped them both. Through Rob Hackwill, she was trying to tell herself something, trying to understand a mystery.

Duroc, unconscious, was heavy and awkward. He came round while she was binding him, but did not struggle or try to talk.

It was not over.

When she was finished with Duroc, she checked on Jerome. He was breathing but asleep. She sat, exhausted and shivering, against a bulkhead. Duroc watched her, as inexpressive as ever.

'The Lord's work,' he repeated.

She tried to stop her teeth chattering.

For the first time in fifteen years, the Reverend Joseph Model was unavailable for comment.

In the Castle, Czech I-Pol interrogated the accused. Chantal and Jerome stood in the dark beyond the mirror, watching. Duroc was co-operative, giving convincing detail. He had precise recall of what he claimed were 156 homicides going back to 2010. He insistently referred to 'the Lord's work' and respectfully claimed that the Lord's needs were revealed to him by the teachings of the Reverend Model.

'I say, he's going to be a Model Prisoner,' snorted Jerome.

Through one-way glass, Duroc seemed to be looking at her. He explained how he had schooled Hugh Best to make a confession, claiming five murders. He took no delight in his crimes but was punctilious in corroborating his claims. She was sure even a cursory check would confirm everything he said.

Jerome's forehead was disfigured by a splotch of hardened healing gel. He was certainly taking his knocks.

She was all right, but her shoulders felt as if she had been racked and her back was scraped raw. She was a real Tina. She had faced the monster and won. She would be around for the sequel.

All her hurt was inside.

Rob Hackwill was laughing in her dreams, exulting in a victory she did not yet understand. And his Devil Princess whispered to her. She sometimes looked like Stacey, sometimes like Beth Yatman. And sometimes, horribly, like Chantal Juillerat, S.J.

'It was too easy,' Chantal said. 'He got away with it for too long to be stopped by us.'

'He doesn't seem upset or unhappy.'

Duroc politely refused an offer of recaff or a cigarette. His faith required him to abjure stimulants. He explained the electro-magnetic pulse he had used to mindwipe Allan Keyes. Model called the Talent 'the author of Maximum Evil', and Duroc had been the instrument of the Lord's vengeance.

'This is like everything else he ever did. Part of his program.'

*

The ghetto was clear of Modelists. Prague was pacified for the moment, at the expense of armoured EDF goons on every corner. As Eunion servants, Chantal and Jerome would have priority when travel restrictions were lifted. For every week their flights were delayed, they were given McDonald's scrip redeemable for a Happy Meal at any airport in the world.

They were alone on the *Meyrink*. The EDF Rapid Response team was re-deploying to Dublin, where the factionalised followers of so-called Anti-Pope James Bacon were fire-bombing each other.

Duroc was all over the newsnets, nick-named 'the Scourge of God', 'Model's Murder Messiah' or 'Holy Hackwill'. He was likely to end his days in the Eunion Penal Therapy Colony on Sicily, shackled in an *oubliette*. Pyramid announced a drama-docudream about his killing spree.

In Broadmoor, Beth Yatman changed her plea from 'Hackwill made me do it' to 'God told me to'. In Kiev, the Relatives of Hackwill Victims – reconstituted as the Relatives of Victims of Religious Fanaticism – changed their lawsuit. Pyramid Releasing and Derek Leech Enterprises were no longer indicted. The new defendants were Reverend Joseph Model, the Modelist Tele-Ministry and the State of Liechtenstein.

If, under the Model-Duff Law, the case was decided in the favour of RVRF, Model and his church would be bankrupt, forced to bestow settlements on upwards of 25,000 claimants. Purge survivors all over the Eunion were bringing their own suits against Model.

All because of Roger Duroc.

Jerome importuned her for spiritual advice she could not give. Her own faith was not shaky, but she sensed a precedent: if religions were responsible legally for violence done in God's name, what church would still stand in ten years time?

On the deck of the *Meyrink*, she walked with Jerome. Suddenly, he kissed her.

'That was for coming out of the river for me. I've never thanked you.'

'I don't think Duroc would have killed you.'

'That's not what either of us thought then.'

She had been going over Duroc's bio, following everything that came out on the newsnets. It was important that she understand. It was the same old question: what makes a monster of a man?

'It started in the Basque Insurrection,' she thought out loud. 'He saw what the Modelists were capable of in that carnage, then joined their church.'

'He was a murderer. Modelism was made for him.'

'He wasn't a murderer then. He didn't kill – even in battle – until after he joined the church.'

'Model brought out something in him. Medea Calm was right. The Reverend should have looked to his own house. The Amendment is based on the theory that people can be warped by mediamass, that dreaming of Hackwill turns you into him. Duroc proved the theory sound, but established we did not have to worry about what came out of the mind of Allan Keyes but what we heard in the pulpit and read in the Bible. You can weigh fifteen supposed Hackwill Killers against thousands of murderers who fancy themselves instruments of a vengeful God. They all learned madness in a church somewhere.'

'Exactly. And I intuit that's the position Duroc wants us to take. Or, worse, the truth he wants us to face. He's spent ten years and 156 lives on his design. And he's going to bring down a church that could count itself among the world's great powers.'

'Your lot will probably canonise him.'

'If God's ministers can be brought to trial for the crimes of His followers, Modelism will only be the first church to fall.'

This morning, Cardinal Menzies had reported that the first lawsuits were being laid against the Vatican. RVRF expanded their claims, charging not only Modelists but seventeen other major churches. Georgi was not handling the impending crisis well. Menzies wanted her in Vatican City. She was their expert on what made people murder.

It began to rain, gently at first.

'I was once told raindrops were God's tears,' Jerome said. 'He has a lot to cry about.'

Prague rain was rusty, laced with pollutants from seventy-five years of unregulated factory smokestacks. The Vlatava was choppy today. The deck shifted under them.

She took Jerome's hand. She needed human contact, something to fix on, some outward manifestation of God's goodness. Though His servants were flawed, Creation was a marvel.

'I'm afraid, Jerome...'

'Chan?'

'Churches are built on corpses. Mine most of all.'

If Kiev upheld Model-Duff, the great wealth of the Roman Catholic Church – of all churches within the Eunion – was in peril. There were incalculable economic consequences.

'I liked him, Chan. I thought he liked us. Despite all the pegs and abjuring, I truly intuited he was a solid fellow. Was he really mad all along?'

'He was trying to teach us a lesson. Maybe he would have had to be mad to try. Maybe, after all, there was a little of Rob Hackwill in him. It's all been about attributions of guilt. It's all been about where the bodies are buried.'

She gripped Jerome's hand until her knuckles hurt. Soon, she would let go, let him go, let Duroc go, let Hackwill go. Soon, she would return to Rome, to her cell, to her faith, to fighting for her church.

Soon.

The rain began to pelt. Drops drummed the deck like liquid bullets, driving them below.

DRAMATIS PERSONAE

Robert Hackwill
Life's Lottery
Reg Jessup
Life's Lottery
The McKinnell Brothers
Life's Lottery
Allan Keyes
The Quorum
Ray Calme
'Out of the Night When the Full Moon is Bright'
Ellen Jeanette Sheridan
'Out of the Night When the Full Moon is Bright'
Breeze Brasselle
The Quorum
Muldoon Pezz
'Out of the Night When the Full Moon is Bright'
Elizabeth Yatman
Jago, Life's Lottery
Derek Leech
'The Original Dr Shade', 'SQPR', 'Organ Donors', *The Quorum, Life's Lottery,*
Seven Stars: 'Mimsy', *Seven Stars:* 'The Dog Story',
Seven Stars: 'Duel of the Seven Stars'
Morag Duff
'SQPR', *The Quorum*
Inspector Joe Hollis
Bad Dreams
Barry Gatlin
The Quorum
WPC Stacy Cotterill
Jago, The Quorum
Ariane
'The Next-But-One Man'
Chantal Juillerat S.J.
Demon Download
Jerome Rhodes
'Organ Donors', *The Quorum, Life's Lottery,*
Seven Stars: 'Mimsy', *Seven Stars:* 'The Dog Story',
Seven Stars: 'Duel of the Seven Stars'
Roger Duroc
Route 666, Demon Download, Krokodil Tears, Comeback Tour

Shadows of Light and Dark
Jo Fletcher

Stunning poetry by award-winning poet Jo Fletcher

Introduction by Neil Gaiman ("...these [are] snatches of devotion, obsession, lust and pain.")

Cover artwork by Les Edwards. Back cover photo by Seamus Ryan. Designed by Michael Marshall Smith.

Available in a limited, numbered edition (250 copies), signed by all the contributors.

Hardcover with dustjacket. Only £12.99
ISBN 0-9532260-1-8

The Paladin Mandates
Mike Chinn

Damian Paladin is an enigma. He is hero, pilot and ghost hunter. Set in 1930s America, these stories pitch Paladin against river spirits, banshees, the undead, ancient Egyptian curses – and the Mafia. This book mixes dollops of The Shadow, Dominic Fortune, Indiana Jones – and a hint of the *X-Files*. *The Paladin Mandates* collects six stories, including three brand new tales, and is fully illustrated by Bob Covington, including a full-colour cover.

Trade paperback £6.00. ISBN 0-9532260-0-X

Coming soon:

Swords Against the Millennium
Edited by Mike Chinn

Coming from Alchemy Press in 2000, an original anthology of Heroic Fantasy as it used to be: brave heroes, crafty thieves, and powerful mages. Fiction from the finest writers and illustrations from the best artists in the genre today. Included in this anthology will be stories from Ramsey Campbell, Adrian Cole, Simon R. Green, Joel Lane & Lisanne Norman. With artwork from such award-winning artists as Bob Covington & Jim Pitts. The book is to be published in both paperback and limited edition hardback. The hardback edition will be signed by all contributors.

Make cheques and money orders payable to The Alchemy Press, and send to
The Alchemy Press, 46 Oxford Road, Acocks Green, Birmingham, B27 6DT, UK

http://www.alchemypress.demon.co.uk